ESCAPE FROM YUMA

ESCAPE FROM YUMA

Jack Cummings

Walker and Company
New York

AUTHOR'S NOTE

This novel was loosely suggested by an incident in the life of historic Pearl Hart, known in her time as "The Last of the Lady Road Agents." All else is fiction.

First published in the United States of America in 1990 by Walker Publishing Company, Inc.

Published simultaneously in Canada by Thomas Allen & Son Canada, Limited, Markham, Ontario

Library of Congress Cataloging-in-Publication Data

Cummings, Jack
Escape from Yuma / Jack Cummings.
ISBN 0-8027-4111-8
I. Title.
PS3553.U444E8   1990
813'.54—dc20   90-12112
CIP

Printed in the United States of America

2   4   6   8   10   9   7   5   3   1

PROLOGUE

Arizona Territory, April 1887

The northbound stage, on its run from Casa Grande to Globe, had no shotgun messenger because it carried no strongbox. It had no cargo except the three passengers and luggage for two of them. The third had no luggage. He was a Pima Indian.

That made it easy for the boyish figure in the range clothes and half-mask of a bandanna to hold up the stage as the team strained to pull it the last few yards up the long grade.

The team was winded, and that decided the driver, Hap Hanson, against making a downhill run for it. Besides, that slight figure on a dun mare, popping out of the roadside brush, could shoot hell out of him, he was thinking.

Hap halted, staring at the .44 Colt in the bandit's hand. Hap was nervous, because you never knew what one of these damn fool kids might do with a pistol.

"Get down," the kid said, voice high with strain. "And tell the passengers to get out."

Hanson set the brake and clambered from his seat. He called into the coach, "You heard the man. Show yourselves!"

The three passengers, a fat middle-aged drummer, a thin young man dressed like an eastern dude, and the ageless Pima, got out.

Ridge Conley, deputy United States marshal based in Florence, was riding his big gray road horse toward Casa Grande when he came upon the scene. He was a lean, tough man of thirty.

Breaking over the grade summit, he drew up.

There hadn't been a stage robbery in his area for some time. It griped him to see one now.

The youthful-appearing bandit was gathering one-handed some pocket money being held out by the two white passengers.

The Pima, his hands empty, kept them raised high.

Conley dismounted, dropped his reins at road's edge, and moved with quick, silent steps close enough to draw his own Peacemaker and growl, "Drop it, kid!"

The startled bandit dropped the money.

"I mean the gun," Conley said.

The kid dropped the Colt.

"Turn around!"

The kid turned, and Conley studied the effeminate features above the covering of the lower face.

"Pull that neckerchief down."

A slim, strong hand reached up and pulled it loose.

Conley stared. With his left hand he reached out and grabbed the wide-brimmed hat and jerked it loose. There was a cascade of long, light-brown locks.

"So!" he said.

She was silent, showing him a frightened look.

"I've seen you somewhere," he said.

It was as if she couldn't speak.

"Do you know me?" he said.

She nodded. Her eyes flicked to his chest. He wasn't wearing his star, but she said, in a small voice, "You're the U.S. marshal at Florence."

"And you once worked as cook at the White Star mining camp," Conley said. "I recollect seeing you there."

Hanson, who had been standing with his passengers, all of them taking in the conversation, suddenly spoke up. "Conley, it's heartwarming to see the two of you enjoying a reunion. But I ought to be getting on with my schedule."

"You know this girl?" Conley said. She didn't look to be more than nineteen, he thought.

"Of course I know her, now you've tore her mask off. Name of Opal. Lived a couple of months in Globe after she married a tinhorn gambler name of Hartman." Hap paused. "Opal Hartman. Been a cook, worked a spell as waitress in a restaurant in Globe after Hartman deserted her." He stopped and said to Opal, "What the hell got into you, girl, to try to rob my stage?"

"I didn't know it was yours till it was too late."

"I mean *any* stage," Hap said. "I always thought you was a good girl."

She did not speak.

Conley said, "Answer the man!"

"What answer can I give?"

"He wants to know why you held up the stage."

"I needed money," she said.

"That's no excuse."

She was silent again, then said, "My mother is dying of consumption. Up in Colorado. Her doctor wrote me that her only hope is to be put in a sanitarium. I've sent what money I could, but it isn't enough."

"Hell," Hanson said, "the passengers have got their money back. Why not let her go, Marshal?"

Conley did not answer at once. Then, slowly, he said, "It doesn't work that way with lawbreakers. They get away with their first crime, and the next time they need money, they try it again."

"She ain't much more than a kid," Hap said. "And a fine-looking girl she is. Ask the passengers here if they want to see her jailed."

The fat drummer said, "I don't, Marshal. I got my money back."

The Pima said, "I never had no money. So I didn't lose nothing."

"See?" Hap said.

"Just a minute, now," the eastern dude said petulantly. "I differ. I agree with the marshal. She broke the law, she should be punished. And I will do my best to see she is."

"How?" Hap said.

"There are other authorities to appeal to, and the marshal knows that. Letting a bandit go, who he caught red-handed, that would be an outrageous offense!"

"That bother you, Marshal?" Hap said.

The girl looked at Conley with hopeful eyes.

"I'm sworn to uphold the law," Conley said. "I've always done so. The only way I know is to bring in those who defy it. I don't judge. The court does that."

"You got a heart of stone, Conley," Hanson said.

"Comes from the job I do," Conley said. He turned to the girl. "You'll ride your mare into Florence with me, miss."

"She could ride in the coach," Hap said.

"Better my way," Conley said. "Not that I don't trust you, Hap."

CHAPTER 1

IN the Florence jail, she first realized the terror that incarceration caused her. Never before had she been locked up. Never before had she been confined to a cage. She had read somewhere of a condition known as claustrophobia, but she had not been aware that she was susceptible to it.

Now she knew how a caged wild animal must feel.

She was driven to behave as one, pacing endlessly the small cell from wall to wall. Seeking, in such action, some release from the terrible feeling of being smothered.

It was a new and dread experience. She had grown up on a Colorado cattle ranch, an outdoor girl, free to ride and roam, and now she was certain she would go mad in confinement.

Being alone, the other cells in the jail empty, only aggravated her.

And then, on the third day, the marshal who had brought her in came to see her.

She should have hated him, and she was shocked when she did not.

Maybe it was because he was the first visitor she'd had, aside from the jailer who shoved a tin plate of food under the barred door twice each day.

He appeared with the jailer, and stood watching her until she noticed him and stopped pacing. There was a somber expression on his ruggedly handsome face.

The jailer, Jeb Collier, said, "She never stops that walking back and forth, Marshal."

Conley said, "Let me in."

5

"Sure," Jeb said. "You want to give me your gun, Marshal? That's the rule for visitors."

Conley gave him a steady look. "You think she's big enough to take it away from me?"

Collier looked uneasy. "Well, no, that ain't likely, you being of half again her size. Still, I might have to answer to the sheriff, was I to bend the rules."

Conley drew his gun and handed it to Jeb.

Jeb unlocked the cell. "Sing out when you're finished," he said.

Conley went in and heard the lock turn behind him.

The girl and he stared at each other.

"What do you want?" she said.

"I just wanted to see how you were taking the lockup."

"Not well," she said. "I'll go crazy if they keep me here very long."

"You'll get used to it."

"Never!" she said. "I can't stand being shut up like this."

He was silent, thinking about this, putting himself in her place. Suddenly he felt the crampedness of the cell himself. He knew there were people who had an irrational fear of tight places. It must be hell, he thought, to be like that and be locked up.

"They say a person can stand almost anything," he said.

"I hope you're right. But I'm not sure I believe it."

"It may not be for long," he said. "Your trial is set for next week."

"Don't I get a lawyer?"

"A county-paid defense attorney will be stopping in later today. I looked him up to find out. Name of Ira Ross. I had a long talk with him."

"Why the interest on your part?" She had seated herself on the edge of the steel bunk.

"Why, I don't rightly know," he said. "I don't usually involve myself once I bring somebody in. I do my job and forget about it. But in your case, I can't seem to do that."

"I suppose I ought to feel flattered," she said. "But I don't." She looked at him without expression. "Will you be at the trial?"

"Of course. I have to testify about your arrest. I have to describe the details of your offense."

"I was a damned fool, Marshal," she said. "I can't, for the life of me, understand why I ever did such a thing. Worry over my sick mother, I suppose. But even so, I find it hard to believe I did it."

"In my business," he said, "I've seen a lot of people do things they regretted. For more reasons than one."

"Do you think I might get off?"

"Would you believe me if I said I hope so?"

"Then why did you arrest me?"

"I thought I explained that to you while I was bringing you in. It was my job."

"Yes," she said. "And I guess I understood then. But being crammed up in this cell makes my understanding weaker now."

"I'm sorry."

"I'm sorrier," she said.

The trial was held in the Pinal County Courthouse on April 29, 1887.

During the days of awaiting it, Opal had become known in the frontier press as "Arizona's Lady Stage Bandit". In less than a week, via the telegraph, she was famous.

And when Hap Hanson leaked word that she had, in desperation, resorted to crime only to save the life of her dying mother, she acquired sympathy as well. With the press and with the spectators who filled the courtroom.

It was a warm afternoon.

Opal was seated beside her appointed defense attorney, Ross. He had seen that the male attire in which she was arrested had been replaced. She now wore the modest dress of a working girl.

Its long sleeves and high collar made her perspire slightly, but it also gave her an appearance of vulnerability, which was the effect that Ross was after.

Promptly at two o'clock, the county prosecutor, Bruce James, presented his case to the all-male jury.

"On trial here," he said, "we have a young woman who did commit a serious offense in violation of the laws of this Territory. To wit, she robbed the passengers of the Casa Grande–Florence stagecoach."

"It is the contention of the prosecution that she should be found guilty and a reasonable penalty be placed upon her to deter her from future crime. . . ."

Defense Attorney Ross did not look displeased. He leaned close to Opal and whispered, "He's not going to be too hard on you, I think. He knows you've got public sympathy, and there's an election coming up."

She did not share his optimism. She had been watching Judge Kane, and saw he was scowling at the prosecutor.

Kane turned his head suddenly and met Opal's glance. She thought she saw venom in his stare.

Conley, seated a row back on the opposite side, saw Kane's scowl too, and was bothered by it.

He had occasionally had a drink with Kane in a local saloon, and now remembered bits of conversation that indicated the judge's antisuffragist leanings. More than that, Kane at times seemed to be antiwomen in general. In fact, Conley thought, the old bastard could well be a misogynist, or whatever it was they called a woman-hater.

Bruce James was again speaking. "I now call to the witness stand the arresting officer."

Reluctantly, Conley arose and went forward.

"Identify yourself, please."

"Deputy United States Marshal Ridge Conley."

"Marshal Conley, please describe the incident on which you based the arrest of the accused."

"I was riding my horse along the Casa Grande–Florence road when I came upon an attempted holdup of the stage."

"*Attempted* holdup?"

"Yes, I would term it that."

"Continue."

Ridge went on to describe the details of what took place. He tried to make them sound the least disfavorable to Opal as he could.

All the while he was doing so, he could feel Judge Kane's eyes drilling into him from the bench.

When he had finished, James said, "You may step down."

Conley wanted to glance across the room at Opal, but controlled the impulse. At the moment, it did not seem wise.

Prosecutor James began calling his witnesses.

The first was the fat drummer. He was perspiring heavily.

"Tell us what happened," James said.

The drummer described the incident, pretty much as Conley had. He hesitated, then said, "Hell, she didn't do us no harm. We got our money back. I say drop the charge."

Judge Kane said, "Another comment like that, and you'll be charged yourself! You are on the stand to present factual evidence, not to offer opinions." He turned to the jurors. "The jury will ignore that outrageous opinion of the witness."

James said quickly to the drummer, "Step down."

The drummer was followed by the eastern dude, who immediately began his recital by referring to Opal as "that low woman."

"I object!" Defense Attorney Ross said. "The witness is voicing his opinion!"

"Objection overruled!" Judge Kane said. "The witness will continue." He was smiling.

"I was frightened to death by that terrible woman," the dude said.

There was a burst of wild laughter from among the spectators.

The Judge rapped his gavel against his bench until it stopped. "There will be no laughing in this court," he said. "The witness will proceed."

The dude rambled on, twisting the details. "She threatened to kill us all if we didn't hand over our money," he said. "I have always heard it said that the female of the species is the most deadly, and now I irrevocably believe it!"

There was another titter from the crowd, squelched instantly by the pounding of Kane's gavel.

"Step down," James said before the dude could resume his tirade.

Hap Hanson took the stand. "I have knowed Opal Hartman for some time," he said before he could be stopped, "and she is a hardworking, honest young woman. I say she caused no harm to none of us, and that had ought to be took into consideration."

Kane was beating with his gavel furiously.

"Hanson," he said, "you are in contempt of this court by violating my orders to adhere to the facts!"

"Facts is what I'm saying," Hap said.

"You know what I mean!" Kane shouted. "I ought to sentence you to jail for contempt."

"Hell," Hanson said, "who'd drive the stage?"

Prosecutor James broke in, saying to Hanson, "Tell us what happened at the scene of the alleged crime."

"The same thing happened that the marshal and that drummer feller said," Hap said. "That dude, though, he's a lying bastard."

"Tell us in your own words," James said, glancing uneasily over his shoulder at the judge. Kane's face was red.

Hap's own words were a match for the drummer's. He had barely finished when Kane broke in from the bench. "Step down!"

There was grumbling from the crowd. It stopped as Opal's attorney got up to address the jurors.

Briefly he incorporated the opinions of the favorable witnesses into his summing-up, ending with a plea for leniency for "this remorseful young lady, who made a first and only mistake out of desperation to save the life of her dying, widowed mother."

Two or three of the men in the jury brushed a hand over their eyes as he finished.

He did not put Opal on the stand, resting his case.

A few moments later, the jury filed out to the deliberation room at the rear of the courtroom.

Fifteen minutes later, they returned.

Judge Kane gave them a studying look. "Have you reached a verdict?"

"We have, Your Honor," the foreman said, standing. He was one of those who had brushed away tears after the defense counsel's plea.

"Well, let's have it," Kane said.

"We find the defendant not guilty as charged," the foreman said.

A cheer rose from the spectators.

The judge's gavel hammered on his benchtop, fit to split it. His face was contorted with rage. "Quiet!" he kept shouting. "Quiet in this court!"

It took a while, but finally the courtroom grew silent. The spectators had quieted as they became curious about what was going on at the judge's bench.

Kane and the prosecutor were in an arm-waving conference of some sort.

Those nearest eventually could hear the words of the discussion.

Judge Kane was saying, "I am telling you that I want a rearraignment of this case. And I want it *now*."

"On what charge?" the prosecutor said.

"I told you, on a charge of *attempted* robbery."

"It'll take time to draw it up, Your Honor."

"Get stared on it, then. I want a trial on this within an

hour. And I'm holding this court on a recess for only that period."

Kane raised his hand then, brandishing it like a fist at the crowd. All at once, there was no noise at all.

"This court is in recess for exactly one hour. Jurors will remain in their box. Counsel for both sides will return at the end of recess. This trial will resume on a new charge against the defendant. That's all!"

He stood up then and retreated to his chambers.

Conley strode over to intercept the prosecutor, who was heading for his own office in the courthouse.

"How can he do that?" he said.

"Don't know of any law against it, though it may be a little irregular," the attorney said. "Look, I've got to live with Kane. Work with him, is what I mean. Let me get on with what I've got only an hour to do."

Conley stood for a moment where he was as the prosecutor rushed off. Then he went over to where Opal still sat, staring disconsolately at her defense counsel. Ross seemed frozen to where he'd stood when objecting to the judge's order to the prosecutor.

Exactly one hour later, the bailiff sang out in his stentorian tones, "This court is now in session. Judge Emil Kane presiding!"

Judge Kane came in and took his place on the bench.

Every eye in the courtroom was fixed on him.

He immediately addressed the jurors.

"You men are here and now specifically instructed to render a verdict on a charge of *attempted* robbery of the Casa Grande–Florence stage passengers. You are to base that verdict strictly on the evidence previously presented to this court before its recess."

"And you are to render said verdict without regard to any personal sympathies for the defendant, or for her womanly wiles of demeanor or physical attributes that may have turned your damned fool heads."

He paused for that to sink in, then said, "I hope you understand my meaning. And remember, I will be sitting on this court for a long time to come."

The jury foreman licked his lips. There was an implied threat there, he thought. A threat for any of them who might be brought before the judge as a defendant in the future.

The jury went out. And once again they returned within a quarter hour.

"Have you reached a *proper* verdict?" Kane said to the foreman.

"Yes, Your Honor." The foreman looked up at Kane, saw the latent threat in his eyes, and dropped his glance. He swallowed nervously.

"Well?"

"We, the jury, find the defendant guilty as charged," the foreman said.

Judge Kane smiled. "The defendant will rise and stand before this bench," he said.

Opal arose unsteadily, stood as if to regain lost balance, then moved slowly forward.

"You have heard the verdict," Kane said. "And now it is my duty to pronounce sentence on you for your crime.

"For attempting to rob the defenseless passengers of the Casa Grande–Florence stagecoach of their hard-earned money, I hereby sentence you to the Territorial Prison at Yuma for a term of five years."

She stood there, stunned.

"That," Judge Kane said, "ought to break you of the habit of robbing stagecoaches for a living."

A groan of protest welled from the courtroom listeners.

"This court is now adjourned," Kane said, and retreated hurriedly to his chambers.

Ridge Conley, too, was stunned. Ever since he'd done his

duty as a law officer by bringing her in, he'd been haunted by regret.

And now someone unidentified in the crowd added to his anguish by yelling, "Conley, you're a real horse's ass!"

CHAPTER 2

Arizona Territorial Prison at Yuma, July 1888

THE thought was always with her. She had to get out. The tiny cell, one of many carved into the hard caliche that comprised Prison Hill, suffocated her. It was worse than the Florence jail, by far.

She had been raised on that Colorado ranch before her father lost his holdings to a powerful eastern-operated cattle company. She was a woman of the wide-open spaces. That spell of first fear, waiting her trial in Florence, had been a warning.

But never had she suffered as she had these many months in this hellhole of a prison. Here, it went beyond unreasoning fear. It reached abject terror that brought panic bordering on madness to her.

Had they not unlocked the cells during the day so that she and the others could pace the small women's yard and look through the wire mesh fence that separated them from the men convicts in the larger compound, she would have gone raving mad long before her first year had passed.

Few men had ever escaped from the Yuma Penitentiary. And no woman, ever.

It was something the prison superintendent brought up whenever he made his "welcome" speech to a new arrival.

"Can you swim?" he'd say.

And if the convict nodded, he'd say, "That's the mighty Colorado River out there, curving around our hill. And as it curves it narrows, and that makes the current too strong for any swimmer to survive."

Then he'd say, "Behind us and on either side stretches the Gran Desierto all the way to Mexico and far beyond."

And if the convict thought, *I have crossed deserts before,* the superintendent would read his mind and say, "You have never seen a desert like this one. No white man—or woman—could survive it, not without a pack mule of provisions and water."

Sometimes a newly arrived prisoner would say, "But I'm not a white man." He might be an Indian or a Mexican.

Then the superintendent would say, "So! I guess the guards on the walls with their Winchester 44-40's will have to watch you closer."

And then he'd grin, and the new convict would know he'd ought to have kept his mouth shut.

So she had been here a year. A year and a couple of months.

Four more years to go, she thought. The thought alone was too much to bear. The terrible, unreasoning fear began to strangle her.

I would welcome the desert, she thought. *I will risk it, if ever I get the chance. I would rather die out in the open than live here confined.*

I'm like an Indian in that regard, she thought. She had heard that Indians often died if they were jailed for long periods of time. Was that true, or was it just another myth? she wondered.

There were some Indians here, and she would ask one next time she found one staring at her through the fence.

One Indian in particular stuck in her mind. He was new.

He was young, and taller than most, and had interestedly looked at her and smiled, more than once, though he had made no lascivious remarks as some of the others had.

The Mexican inmates were the worst for that, she thought. They lusted for her and the three other women now serving time.

It was to be expected, of course. A natural thing. But the Mexican men accompanied their fine white smiles with obscene remarks that enraged her. The three other women were Mexican, and seemed more flattered than shocked.

"Love talk, Opal," one of them told her. "It is only their way of making love."

The tall Indian—was he Pima, a younger version of the one on the stage she had so foolishly tried to rob?—he was courteous, she thought. At least he so impressed her. A handsome man, too, in his Indian sort of way.

She spoke to one of the Mexican women about him. "That tall Indian who smiles at us sometimes . . . Is he Pima?"

The woman, Dorotea, grinned. "You like him, eh?"

"I asked a question, that's all."

"Sure, you ask. Somewhere I hear he is Quechan."

"Quechan? Aren't they the ones who sometimes bring back men who have escaped?"

"Sure, they know the desert more better than anybody. The *jefe* of the prison, he pay them fifty dollars reward to bring one back."

"Fifty dollars?"

Dorotea grinned again. "You thinking of something besides how looks that tall *indio,* eh, Opal? But you think of this, it is fifty dollars, dead or alive."

"But he is himself a convict."

"Sure. So now he inside instead of out."

"You think he knows the desert?"

"Maybe."

"Only some Quechans know." Dorotea paused. "You got loco idea inside your head, Opal?"

"No," Opal said. "I'm just talking."

"You think about get out," Dorotea said, "you better think about dead or alive."

Opal made no reply to that.

"That tall Quechan, Mexican name for his is Pascual. He is

muy bonito for an *indio*, no?" Dorotea said. "Me, I like to think about him, too."

There was another convict who came occasionally to the women's fence to stare at Opal. He was a hard-looking white man, tanned almost to the shade of the *indio*.

During the several months he had been there, she had learned something about him too.

His name was Sam Fannin, and she recalled hearing his name mentioned in the past. He had a fame of sorts as a rustler and gunman. He, too, was doing a five-year sentence. On a rustling conviction, his first. He was in his late twenties, she judged, with a sinewy build that fit his weathered complexion.

When he looked at her, he too smiled, but only faintly. It was a smile that disturbed her. He had never spoken to her and that made her wonder if his smile was a threat.

And now, two months into the second year of her incarceration, she despaired that she would ever get out. It was July, and the heat was already topping 110 degrees at midday. What would it be out there on the Great Desert? she wondered. A woman alone would undoubtedly die.

And why worry about the desert? she thought, her eyes sweeping the tops of the thick adobe walls, sixteen feet about the compound.

The walls, it was said, were eight feet thick at their base, five at their top.

And the top formed a walkway for patrolling guards, armed with Winchesters and handguns. And at each corner was a guard tower, equally manned.

And then one day, even as she despaired, six of the male convicts attempted a breakout.

It began as Superintendent Robert Bates crossed the main yard toward the sally port exit to his bungalow residence outside the walls.

A prisoner named Sanchez, who regularly worked in the shoe shop, stepped out to accost him, complaining that he had not been let out of his cell as early as he should be, and that since he was anxious to learn the trade of shoemaking, he wanted to know the reason why.

"I have no idea," Bates, said, but since Sanchez had always been a model prisoner, he added, "I'll look into the matter for you."

"*Gracias, jefe,*" Sanchez said, and smiled, as Bates entered the thick, arched exit.

At that moment he was grabbed by two inmates.

"Are you men crazy?" Bates said.

One of them, named Stevenson, said, "Sorry, Bates. But we're getting out, and there are others with us in this. All you got to do is escort us to the brush along the river and order any guards that spot us not to fire. You do that and you won't get hurt." He paused. "But if anyone of us is hurt, you're going to die. You understand?"

Bates was no fool. He nodded.

Outside the iron-barred double gate, the gatekeeper stepped out of his little shack and stared in at them.

"Open up," Bates said.

The turnkey looked dubious, but obeyed.

Immediately three other convicts pushed by and rushed out toward the superintendent's cottage. The yardmaster, Fraser, appeared, unarmed, and one of the convicts, who was carrying a pick handle, swung at him.

Fraser ducked, grabbed the club, and tried to tear it loose.

In the struggle, both men fell over a steep embankment adjoining the house.

The assistant superintendent, in his own residence nearby, was aroused by the disturbance. He grabbed a rifle from a rack and stepped outside.

He yelled down at the man still struggling with Fraser, "Come up with your hands high!"

The convict let got of Fraser, stared at the assistant with

bitter eyes, then began a slow climb up the embankment, holding his hands awkwardly above his head.

Seeing the armed assistant, another convict panicked and ran around the north side of the superintendent's house toward the river. A guard named Miller, on the catwalk of the north wall, halted him with a single shot.

A third inmate ran south down Penitentiary Road. He was spotted by Guard Randall, stationed on the southwest corner of the perimeter. Randall fired, and the man slid over a bank out of range, but with blood spurting from his upper torso.

Convict Stevenson, unarmed and stalemated in the sally port, frisked Bates for a weapon and found none. Stevenson seemed now undecided what to do.

Two convicts came out of the superintendent's house, carrying pistols.

One of them was shot down by Guard Hall from on top the northeast section of the wall.

The other, inexplicably, sprinted for the sally port, Hall shooting up dust spurts behind him.

He reached the port and leveled his weapon at Bates. Bates knocked it aside with his hand. It discharged, hitting Stevenson in the left arm.

The assistant superintendent fired across the residence compound at the convict with the gun, and dropped him.

The other convict in the port, unarmed, spooked and ran out into the open, hands held high. He called to the assistant superintendent, "Don't shoot! Don't shoot!"

Guard Hall shot him.

Stevenson, enraged, pulled a butcher knife from his belt and drove it into Bates's neck where it joined his shoulder. He drove it with such force that it carried both of them out of the port and into the open.

Bates fell, pulling the knife handle free of Stevenson's grip.

Guard Hall shot Stevenson in the head.

It was over. Four of the convicts were killed. The one shot

down by Guard Randall lay bleeding with two bullet wounds. The sixth, who'd tangled with Yardmaster Fraser, had given up.

Superintendent Bates, in acute pain and bleeding profusely, was rushed to the infirmary.

His one thought at this time was, *Thank God that's the end of it!*

But it wasn't.

Because even as the attempted breakout began, Pascual the tall Quechan, who had known it was coming, was at the separation fence of the women's yard and calling to Opal. He had spoken to her many times lately, close conversations through the fence.

Now he said, "Is time we go!" He had learned only fair English somewhere, she thought.

Adrenaline shot through her. And hope. It was this she had been waiting for. It was this they had furtively discussed for weeks now, and always he had said, "Wait."

She had chafed, living with her dread of confinement. Yet it was this terrible, suffocating fear that had determined her to risk whatever she might undergo at his hands once they were free.

Such was the senseless phobia she endured that she would risk his lust—and she knew this would be his reason for helping her to escape. It would be his price.

Once out, she thought, she would have to deal with him.

He was reaching for her now, his long, strong arms extending high to clear the fence top. She caught his hands, and he lifted as she toed her way up the fence links partway.

As she toppled forward, he dragged her roughly over the top. Her thin prison jacket did not protect the hurt to her breasts, and she cried out, but he ignored it.

He dropped her to the ground, then rushed with her along the inside of the west prison wall, keeping close to it so the guard above would, they hoped, take no notice.

They reached the northwest corner and turned east along the inside of the north wall, shielded somewhat by the rectangular shops building an arm's distance away.

There now was the sally port, a few yards beyond.

Pascual abruptly halted as the assistant superintendent and the gatekeeper suddenly appeared from the port half carrying the wounded Bates. They moved awkwardly toward the main building, which housed the infirmary.

The guards atop the walls were all staring at the trio from their vantage points, intent on the seriousness of the superintendent's wound.

God, don't let them see us, Opal thought. *Let them keep looking elsewhere.*

Her plea appeared to be answered.

And then the gatekeeper for some reason turned his head and looked down the narrow passage in which she and the Quechan crowded.

They were in the shadows, and he was moving fast, and she held her breath. Then he was out of sight, and she waited, expecting him to call out.

There was no call, and her relief was so great that she lost the will to move.

Pascual was tugging at her now. "Come!" he said. He pulled her along toward the vacated sally port.

And at that moment, from a rear door of the shop building, Sam Fannin stepped out in front of them. He had a pair of canteens cross-slung from either shoulder.

"Might was well make it a threesome," he said, and immediately led off.

They reached the sally port and ducked in. The convict killed by the assistant superintendent still lay there, his sprawled body hiding the gun he held in his hand. Fannin and Pascual bumped as they stepped over him, knocking each other reeling.

As they straightened up, their eyes met in a brief stare. Fannin's eyes were as black as the Indian's. Both stares were obsidian hard. Opal thought, seeing this, that there could be bad trouble ahead between them.

Fannin broke off his stare. "That guard Hall was watching Bates cross the yard. Let's hope he still is."

"Which way, then?" Pascual said.

"To the right, east, along the wall, past the tank, over the bluff. Then we head south into the desert."

"We now go!" the Quechan said.

They went, moving fast. Opal swept a glance across the outside compound as Pascual led her again by the hand. It appeared empty for the moment except for three sprawled dead bodies in convict's garb.

She shuddered. Her glance could not tell who they were. But she would have known them, at least by sight. Fellow inmates in this hellhole. The thought struck her then that it was their dying that had given her this chance.

I will not let it be a waste, she thought.

It was a God-given opportunity, and no matter what she faced ahead, it could not be worse than what she had been undergoing.

Panic gripped her that she might be quickly recaptured. She and her confederates had a long way to go before they could count themselves free.

Her panic caused her to speak now. She addressed Pascual, because he was the one she considered a friend. Fannin was a stranger, an intruder, even though she had seen him many times through the fence.

"Hurry," she gasped to Pascual. She was right on his heels.

The Quechan did not speak, did not change his pace.

Behind her, Fannin said, "It's a long run ahead, to shake those guards. We got to pace ourselves, especially with you along."

"I can keep up," she said, breathing hard. "What good is pacing if they are right behind us?"

"I don't think they are. Not yet. That shoot-out in the yard has got them confused."

"They won't be for long," she said.

"It gives us a chance to put some distance between us. And, girl, you'll be the one left behind if it comes to a flat-out footrace and you can't keep up."

She believed that. Fannin would abandon her quick enough if it was needed to ensure his own escape.

She wasn't sure what Pascual would do.

CHAPTER 3

RIDGE Conley caught the westbound Southern Pacific train at Casa Grande, destination Yuma.

There he got a ride up Prison Hill on a supply wagon. The teamster, a curious oldster, white of beard, eyed him well before accepting him as a passenger.

Sensing his reservations, Conley pulled his star from a pocket and pinned it on his shirt.

"That's different," the teamster said. "Get aboard!"

He drove in silence for a short spell, then said, "Feller can't be too careful nowadays. I mean, after what happened a couple of days ago up in the pen."

"I understand," Conley said.

The old man gave him a quick glance. "You heard about it, then?"

"Some," Conley said.

"Biggest attempted breakout they ever had so far."

"Not too successful, I heard."

"Not for them that planned it," the teamster said. "One of them convicts that survived the guard's shooting, what he said was it was him and one other and the dead ones that was in on it."

"Figures," Conley said.

"Not the whole of it, though. Three others slipped away during the excitement, you know."

Ridge knew from the telegram he'd received at Florence, but he didn't say so.

"I guess you heard. An Injun called Pascual, a hardcase rustler named Sam Fannin, and that woman stage robber that made all the newspapers a year or so ago."

25

"Opal Hartman," Conley said.

"That's the one. Seems, according to the breakout feller's story, that her and the Injun and Fannin wasn't even in on the plan. They just took advantage of the guards' having their hands full shooting the others, and slipped away without being noticed. They wasn't even missed in the hullabaloo until evening countdown, when they was supposed to go back into them tiny cells."

"Have the guards tried to find them?" Conley said.

"Took a quick look and gave up, I reckon. Them guards can't be spared from their regular duty. Especially now, with all them cons keyed up about the three that got away."

"I guess."

"Besides, them guards are inside men. Hell, they ain't trackers or manhunters."

Conley said, "Yeah."

The oldster looked at him again, and at the star he now wore. "Maybe that's why you're heading up the hill," he said.

"Maybe," Conley said.

The old teamster frowned. Nobody irritated him more than a closemouthed man.

Superintendent Bates's neck was bandaged, and he was showing pain. He could not even hold his head straightly erect. He stared now across his office desk, and Conley could see the suffering in his eyes.

Conley said, "Why me?"

"This thing will have reverberations," Bates said. "An attempted major breakout, with four convicts killed, one wounded, and three escaped, including a woman. In eleven years of this prison's administration, my predecessors never suffered a catastrophe this big."

"They were lucky," Conley said. "You keep men locked up in little holes dug out of a caliche hill, it was bound to happen."

"We try to be humane," Bates said. "They're let out of

their cages during the day—to work on the rockpile, or other duties." He paused, then said, "Dammit! Don't you add to the criticism the newspapers are giving me!"

"I didn't mean to," Conley said.

After a moment, Bates went on, "What makes it all ten times worse is a *woman* escaped."

Conley almost grinned at the outrage in the superintendent's voice. He said nothing.

"And not just *any* woman!" Bates said. "It had to be Opal Hartman, for cripes sake! We've got—had—four females currently in the women's section, and it had to be her."

"The prettiest lady stagecoach robber of them all," Conley said. "The darling of the frontier newspapers and their readers from the time she was first jailed."

"You remember, then?" Bates said.

"Hard to forget," Conley said. "I was the one who jailed her. And overnight I became the most hated deputy U.S. marshal in Arizona, if not the whole West." He paused. "You know, that part about her doing it only to save her poor old mother's life—it turned out to be the truth." He hesitated again, then said, "It turned me into a villain, and made her a heroine throughout the Territory."

Superintendent Bates gave a vigorous nod, then flinched at the pain this caused him. "So you see what happened here isn't likely to blow over. The girl is big news again. And she's out there somewhere—free." He was silent a moment, then said, "And I'm the whipping boy as long as she is."

"So what do you want from me, exactly?" Conley said.

"I want you to bring her back."

It was Conley's turn to nod. "You know, when I got your wire, I intended to ignore it. I had enough of Opal Hartman press to last me."

"Then you got your orders from your superiors," Bates said.

"You must have friends in high places," Conley said.

"A political debt or two was owed me," Bates said.

"Again, I ask, why me?"

"You have a proven record as a top man-tracker," Bates said. "And putting her old nemesis on her trail may take some heat off my own neck. Believe me, this knife wound in the neck gives me agony enough."

"It isn't a job I want to do," Ridge Conley said. "Being the most hated man in the West isn't something I feel comfortable with."

"You may not catch her," Bates said.

"Then, by God, I'll be the laughingstock."

"From your reputation as a dedicated lawman," Bates said, "I'd guess you'd prefer to be hated. I'm relying on that to keep you going."

Conley was silent, thinking about it. Finally, he said, "Which way did they go?"

"What way is there? Into the desert, of course. My guards tracked them to the edge of it."

"The Gran Desierto," Conley said. "I've never been into it. Not likely she has, either. She could die quick out there."

"She and Fannin have got the Indian with them. At least, we suppose they stayed together. And he is Quechan."

"The desert is Quechan country?"

"If it's anybody's. The Mexicans say it belongs to the devil."

Conley gave him an odd stare. "You trying to talk me out of it?"

"Absolutely not! I'm just warning you of what you'll be up against. But you'll go. One, because you've got your orders. And two, because you're Ridge Conley."

"Right now, I wish I wasn't," Conley said.

"The sooner you get started, the better," the superintendent said.

"I've got to get provisioned," Conley said. "A good desert horse, a pack mule. Food, water. Grain for the animals."

"It's all taken care of," Bates said. "I trust you've brought your weapons?"

Conley nodded.

"The rest is waiting for you. Can you start today? I'll have one of the guards show you where the fugitives entered the desert. The trail now is already cold, of course."

Conley's face was grim. "And at this time of year, I reckon that's the only thing out there that is," he said.

"You can be sure of it," Bates said.

He waited until morning to leave. A pair of off-duty guards accompanied him to where they'd given up trying to follow the escapees' tracks.

"Looks like they're heading south, for sure," one of them said.

"Where else?" Conley said. "Mexico would be the logical goal."

"Maybe so," the other guard said. "But you can't ever be sure. They'd know we'd guess that, and maybe head some other direction."

"You good at reading trail sign, Marshal?" the first one asked.

"I've tracked down a few in my time," Conley said. "I do fair, for a white man."

"Bates ought to've tried to get a couple them Apache scouts off San Carlos, maybe, instead of you," the guard said.

"I wish to hell he had," Conley said. "But he had his reasons."

The pair of them turned away. "Good luck, Marshal," one of them said. "If you catch up with them, you try not to harm the girl, you hear? There wasn't none of us at the pen, guard or convict, that wasn't half in love with her. Damn fine-looking female."

Conley scowled. There it was again, the guard's words reminding him of the general public's sentiment.

Angrily, he swung onto the grullo gelding Bates had selected for him and, leading the pack mule, entered the desert.

In the beginning, he had no trouble following their trail. The Indian would have known the futility of trying to hide it.

Their main thought would have been to put distance between themselves and the guards. And the Quechan, at least, would have guessed the prison personnel would have no expertise as trackers.

They went due south, staying distant from the river that veered westerly below Yuma. There were steamboats on the river, and there were inhabitants scattered along its shore.

The Quechan would want to avoid any contact with them. He would know the risk of appearing with a white woman. And it would be only a short time until word of the breakout would travel down the "brush telegraph," alerting the riverside people to the chance of collecting a reward.

They'd head, Conley was sure, for the border.

The girl, had she been alone, would likely have followed the river, since it would have been the easier way, considering terrain and availability of water.

But the Quechan would know better, he thought. If they were to escape into Mexico, they would have to do it the hard way, through the Yuma desert, and the Gran Desierto beyond.

Was the Quechan familiar with what lay ahead? Just being Quechan didn't necessarily mean he was. There were Quechans who clung close to the river all their lives and knew little or nothing at all of that terrible terrain.

If this Quechan—they called him Pascual, Bates had said, after a famous chief of the tribe, noted for his size—had no knowledge of it, he was a fool to plunge into it, Conley thought.

And I am a fool for following him. His own life, ironically, could depend on the competency of the Indian.

Let's hope he is competent, Conley thought. *But not too competent.*

He thought then of the girl. Her life, too, depended on the Indian.

She must have been desperate, from confinement, to risk her life on the behavior of the Indian, he thought. Not many white women would. And then there was that hard case, Sam Fannin, an unknown quantity in relationship to women.

How would *he* treat her? he wondered. Both men had been locked up for a long time. They would each have a long-deprived man's built-up hunger for a woman.

She was almost sure to be raped, Conley thought. Had she weighed that fact when she decided to join in the flight from the prison? Weighed it, and felt she would pay the price?

Or did she act without thought of consequences?

He did not know her well enough to answer. He only knew this added another worry to those he had.

He carried a folded 1886 map of Arizona in his pocket, and now withdrew it and halted to study it.

Off to his left, in the distance, was a southwest-slanting range he identified as the Gila Mountains.

Much closer, but appearing to parallel the range, was a trail leading to the border.

It appeared to him that the Quechan was bisecting the area between the trail to the east and the river to the west, in an almost direct drive for the Sonora boundary. From the map, Conley judged it was about twenty miles away.

A short ride, he thought, but a hell of a long walk in the heat of July. Did they have water? He had to assume they did not.

And at the boundary there was nothing, except possibly a survey monument, with the endless expanse beyond of the Gran Desierto of Mexico.

Maybe the Indian could make it, he thought, but what about the girl?

He looked about him at the shimmering plain of sparse creosote bush and bur sage, and nothing else.

At a distance the heat waves distorted the sight, giving all he saw a wriggling cast. Over a hundred and ten degrees, he judged, and it could get hotter later.

He studied the map again. Below the Gilas, and running the same direction, were the Tinajas Altas. He dimly recalled they were named for the natural rock tanks high on their lower side. The tanks—*tinajas* was the Spanish name for them—sometimes held water caught during the rare cloudbursts that struck the area.

They might or might not be empty at this time of year. And they were at least forty miles away from where he was now halted.

The girl would never make it.

He found himself deeply worried by the thought. It was a worry strange to him. He had pursued many a lawbreaker in his years of wearing a star, but never before had he been concerned over the well-being of his quarry.

It was a concern that had been with him since the beginning, dating from those many months ago when he had surprised her in the act of holding up the stagecoach.

She seemed so out of place doing it.

It showed′ what desperation can drive a man—or a woman—to do, he thought.

He had brought her in because it was his job to do so. But from the time she was jailed, he'd hoped she'd be acquitted. And now, he had to admit to himself wryly, his acceptance of this assignment without heavy protest was greatly due to his fear that another pursuer might harm her, whether deliberately or not.

And there was Sam Fannin, too. Conley had some knowledge of the man's reputation, although they had never met. Fannin had never been convicted of a crime until his current sentence, but there had long been suspicions of his activities on both sides of the border.

Rumor had been around that Sam stole cattle in Mexico and sold them to American ranchers. Rumor, too, that he rustled American beef and drove it down into Sonora, and sometimes Chihuahua, to sell to Mexican *hacendados*.

He had also hired out his gun in a couple of small-scale range wars.

And he'd killed at least three men in gunfights, though he'd been cleared each time, pleading self-defense.

A shady reputation at best, Conley was thinking. Fannin was one to watch out for under any circumstances. He could be damned dangerous if cornered.

Now, not certain that the escapees would strike for the possible water at Tinajas Altas, he continued to follow their tracks. He could not take the chance that the girl might die of thirst.

Their trail continued south. It came to him then that they feared to cut eastward across the desolate and baking expanse. Unlike himself, they would have no map, he supposed. Any hope they had of surviving would depend on the guidance of the Quechan.

May he know! Conley thought. *May he know the desert!*

And if he knows, may they listen to his advice!

The girl would, he was sure. But would Fannin?

Fannin would know the border country far to the east, near Nogales, which was border-jumper country. He might even know it near Sonoita, at half the distance, a hundred and twenty miles away. But it wasn't likely he'd ever tried to drive cattle here, across the Gran Desierto, or across the volcanic nightmare of blasted rock that formed the Sierra Pinacate beyond the Desierto's eastern edge.

No man in his right mind would try *that*.

It was the land of the Sand Papago Indians, or had been in earlier times.

The Spanish explorers, astounded that even *indios* could survive in such desolation, had named them. Los Papagos Areneros, in Spanish.

They were cousins to the Papagos of the Gila country to the north, but they were far more intractable.

The land made them that way; even the Spanish had understood that. They lived on desert rodents, rabbits, reptiles, roots, and cactus. Their life was harsh, not conducive to amiability. And always they worried about the *tinajas* drying up.

Conley knew that much about them. He knew, too, that few, if any, remained in the vicious environment at this late date. Over the years, nearly all had migrated north to mix with their cousins.

In the end, the Gran Desierto had beaten even them.

There was one, though, who had gone back. He recalled hearing about him somewhere.

His name was Carbajal, and he had gone back to the Tinaja of the Papagos, where his forebears had once lived.

The reservation in Arizona had become too crowded, he'd said.

He'd taken his wife and young son with him, and for a time they had lived as his ancestors had.

But he, too, had tired eventually of trying to survive on the wild *camote* roots, and what meager crops he could raise sporadically in that aridness. And he and his wife had returned to the reservation.

Conley did not remember what became of the now grown son.

The thought struck him that Opal would be better off if the Indian with her were a Sand Papago rather than the Quechan.

And then he was brought up startled by his own thinking.

Why was he so concerned about her? Why wasn't he thinking instead of how to recapture her as quickly as possible, and to hell with her welfare?

That was what he'd better do if he was going to get the job done.

CHAPTER 4

SHE was tiring fast. The months of being penned up, with only the pacing of the women's yard for exercise, had taken a toll of her stamina.

The two men held to their steady pace, not pushing, but still she found herself falling behind. *Damn them*, she thought. *They will leave me.*

She called out in anger, "Wait!"

Only then did they look back. It was as if she had been forgotten.

It was the Indian who spoke then. He said to the white man, "We go slower."

"*You* go slower," Fannin said. "Me, I aim to put distance now between me and that prison."

Pascual said, "How well you know this desert?" He stopped then.

Fannin stopped too, cursing. "I know if I keep going south I'll reach the border."

"And then?" Pascual said. "You know where water is?"

Fannin rapped the canteen he was carrying and pointed at the other he had given to Pascual to carry.

"They don't last long," the Quechan said.

"There's got to be some *tinajas* somewhere out there," Fannin said.

"You can find?"

"Maybe."

"Maybe not, too."

Fannin scowled. "Maybe you can't find water either."

"Maybe not," Pascual said. "You make choice. You go alone,

35

fast as you want. Or you go with me and this woman, fast as we want."

"Kind of stuck on her, ain't you?"

"She and me, we go together."

"Lustful, ain't you?"

"And you?"

"Not right now, for God's sake! Right now, I want to get across that border."

"Is no water there."

"How do you know?"

"I been there, couple times."

"When?"

"While back," Pascual said.

"What the hell does that mean?"

"Only water now is maybe at Tinajas Altas."

"How far?" Fannin said.

"Forty, maybe fifty mile."

"You ain't sure?" Fannin said. "You ever been there?"

The Quechan nodded.

"When?"

"While back."

"What direction?" Fannin said.

"East, now."

"Hell, I want to get to Mexico, quick as I can."

"You got choice. Mexico quick, no water. East to them mountains, forty, fifty miles. Them *tinajas* there. Maybe water."

"Maybe? Ain't you sure of nothing?"

"Nothing sure on this desert," Pascual said. "Maybe animals drink them dry. Maybe it don't rain there in a long time."

Opal had caught her breath after hurrying to catch up. "You better listen to him," she said to Fannin. "He's our only chance to get out of this alive."

"I don't trust nothing a damn Injun tells me," Fannin said. "Every place he says he's been has been 'a while back.' He maybe don't know this desert at all."

"Do *you?*"

"Farther east I do."

"Then farther east we better get," she said. "You agree?"

He said, "You may not make fifty miles on these two canteens we got to share."

"You can see that range of mountains where the *tinajas* will be," Opal said. "And he said maybe only forty."

"Can you make forty in this heat? We got half-gallon canteens. Can you make it on a third of that?"

She gave him a hard, determined look. "Can you?"

He was silent, then he said, "But you're a town girl."

"Listen," she said, "I grew up on a cattle ranch. I'm tougher than you think."

He gave her a surprised look.

"I probably know as much about cattle as you do," she said. "Except for how to steal them."

"Well, well," Fannin said. "We get away free, maybe we can be business partners."

"You ready?" Pascual said.

"We're ready," Opal said.

"We go for the *tinajas,*" Pascual said. He led off then in a southeasterly direction. "*Tinajas* at south end of mountains."

The heat got worse.

The three of them were in prison garb, the men in loose-fitting jackets and trousers, striped horizontally. Striped black on yellow because yellow was easier to spot than white if a prisoner got away into the brush.

Opal's jacket and trousers were of blue denim in place of stripes. A concession to her sex, because no woman had ever before escaped.

All three wore prison-issue floppy cloth hats, poor protection against the blistering sun.

They moved in single file, Pascual picking a path whenever creosote bush blocked the direct course he had fixed on the southerly end of the mountains. She followed second, Fannin bringing up the rear.

She kept hoping that Pascual would halt and offer her a drink from the canteen slung over his shoulder.

There it was, a scant three paces away, swinging with his stride, tantalizing her with his every step.

My God! she thought. *Doesn't he* ever *need water?*

But he was Indian, of course.

However Fannin wasn't. It came to her that Fannin was cheating, that he was swigging covertly. Stealing from water that was partly hers. Unreasoning anger made her twist her head, trying to catch him in the act.

"What the hell's the matter?" he said finally. "You afraid you'll lose me?"

"You're drinking our water!" she said.

"You sure?" he said. "You're maybe seeing things that ain't there, girl." His voice softened a little then. "The desert will make you do that sometimes."

"*I* need a drink," she said, and hated herself even as she said it.

"Tell that redskin friend of yours, then," he said. "He's got a crush on you, you know that." He paused. "Better take advantage of it. Time will come when he'll make you pay anyway." He paused again, then said, "I knew you'd need more than your share."

She turned her head away from him and stared straight ahead. She would not beg. Not from Pascual. And definitely not from him.

And then she felt him at her side, brushing against her.

Startled, she half turned and saw him unscrewing the cap of his canteen and proffering it to her.

She met his eyes, and found them unreadable.

"No!" she said.

"Go ahead," he said. "It's time we were friends."

"And the time will come when you'll want to be paid," she said.

"I'm glad you understand that," he said. "Me and that red-skinned bastard ain't no different when it comes to women. But better you owe me than owe him, don't you think?"

"I do not!"

He swished the water around in the canteen. "Nice cool water," he said.

"Cool! In this heat?" It was just something to say.

He swished it again. "Nice *wet* water," he said.

She grabbed the canteen from him and stopped and tilted it to her mouth and drank deeply.

After a second, he snatched it away from her. "That's enough," he said.

At that moment, she hated him enough to kill. Hated him mostly for weakening her resolve.

And now, as she looked ahead, she saw that Pascual had stopped too, and was watching. He stared for a long moment. Then, as she resumed walking, he turned away to trudge again between the creosote bushes.

He had not spoken a word.

That bothered her. She felt guilty for succumbing to her thirst. For taking more than her share of the water. But her unease was more than that; she somehow valued the Quechan's appraisal of her.

A damn Indian, she thought. *And I worry about what he thinks of me.*

He was a fine-looking man, though. Tall and muscular. Taller and stronger than Fannin, who was lean and tanned and tough, but of moderate build.

In a fight, she guessed, Pascual would be the victor. So long as Fannin was unarmed.

That gave her some sense of protection against the rustler. Pascual would shield her against Fannin, she was sure.

Then she thought: *But who can shield me from Pascual?*

She had been briefly married to that worthless Hartman, who had ice water in his veins, was totally without passion.

Still she knew something about what made men tick. She knew that if the three of them survived the desert, one or both of these men would be after her. Fannin had just told her as much.

If they survived. At the moment, that seemed unlikely. It all depended on Pascual. She had to depend on him, like it or not.

She had come to think of him weeks earlier, as her only way out. Back during their discussions through the prison fence. And when he had come for her during the breakout, she had not hesitated to accept his help.

If only Sam Fannin hadn't joined them, she thought. There would be trouble between the two men, perhaps a standoff over her.

Still, Fannin was the one with the foresight to bring water. Without those canteens he had stolen from a work-detail locker, they would never have gotten this far.

She had to face it, then. She needed both men if she was to avoid recapture. At least now, in the early stage of her flight. She would worry later about the consequences. She could only believe they would be considerable.

The stark white mountains, where the *tinajas* were supposed to be, never seemed to get closer. She had walked ten miles, she judged, since Pascual had altered their destination. It was as if they trudged in place, like a squirrel in a tread cage, only slower, much slower, never getting anywhere.

Once Pascual had halted them while they drank sparingly from the canteens.

"How far now?" Fannin said.

"Maybe thirty miles," the Quechan said.

"And two-thirds of our water gone," Fannin said.

"What if the tanks are empty?" Opal asked Pascual.

He looked at her and shrugged. "Then we join other bones piled there."

"It has happened often?"

He nodded.

Suddenly, then, he squinted hard across the shimmering flats.

"What's wrong?"

"You wait," he said, and moved away quickly, soon screened from view by the brush that seemed to grow thicker here.

She did not like to be alone with Fannin.

He had seated himself in the scant shade of a greasewood.

"You had best take a rest, girl," he said.

Doubt tugged at her, and she said, "Suppose he doesn't come back?"

He grinned at the panic in her voice. "You afraid to be alone with old Sam?"

When she did not answer, he said, "He'll be back. He won't leave you until he satisfies his wants."

"How do you know?"

He just grinned, nothing else.

She hated his grin.

He patted the ground beside him. "Rest while you can," he said. "Thirty miles to go."

She ignored his gesture and sought her own shade a distance away.

They sat then in silence.

When she again glanced nervously at him, his grin was gone.

He met her eyes, then said in a tired voice, "Hell, girl, there's a time and place for everything. And, believe me, this ain't it. I'm as near tuckered out as you are, I reckon."

She could think of nothing to say to that.

In a few minutes, Pascual came back.

"What'd you see?" Fannin said.

"Just a trail. Trail from Yuma down to boundary line."

"Hell, we could have taken that a lot easier."

"We been caught by guards maybe, if so."

"Anybody on it now?"

"I don't see nobody."

Fannin said, "Ain't there a trail of sorts goes along the boundary?"

The Quechan nodded. "Old trail, call Devil's Highway by Mexicans. We take trail down there now. It go close to *tinajas* where we want to go."

"What about guards that might still be out looking for us on that trail you found?" Fannin said.

"They gone back by now, I think. Too hot. They don't come this far down."

"What about Injuns?" Fannin said. "Your own kind. I heard they're willing to bring back a prisoner for fifty bucks."

"I don't think my people out here either. Too hot for them too. Fifty dollars not worth it."

"I hope you ain't lying."

"I keep eye open for them. We go now."

Opal said, "Why can't we travel after dark, when the sun is gone?"

"In the dark?" Fannin said. "Walking in this brush? Not me. This time of year, at night, every damned rattlesnake in the Territory is out looking for rodents to eat."

"I forgot," she said.

"By God! I didn't. I been twice bit by the sons of bitches!"

They moved off again.

As they approached the trail down from Yuma, they eyed it carefully. As Pascual had said, there were no travelers. Who the hell would be out here, anyway?

The trail appeared to be infrequently used, although Opal recalled hearing of it somewhere. In earlier days, the Spanish had named it, and later the forty-niners heading for California's gold had sometimes risked it when the Apaches were lying in wait on the Gila River to the north.

"El Camino del Diablo," the Spanish, and later the Mexicans, had called it. The Highway of the Devil. It led across the Gran Desierto from east to west until it turned northwesterly toward the river crossing at Yuma.

It was aptly named, Opal thought, even though she guessed the worst would be ahead.

Those bones Pascual had mentioned, piled at the *tinajas,* would some of them belong to the California gold rushers of '49? she wondered. Tinajas Altas was the single oasis in the long border stretch they had traveled.

And again, she wondered, would it be dry? She racked her mind trying to recall when, if at all, it had rained during these past months. But in a land where a season total averaged two or three inches, the recollection eluded her.

But she was certain it had not rained these past six months at all.

God help us! she thought. *The* tinajas *will be dry.*

Under that blazing brass sky above, how could they be anything else? Not a cloud anywhere, except a thin band on the horizon far, far to the south, somewhere over the Sea of Cortez.

She fell exhausted late in the afternoon of the second day. She was about to die, she was sure.

Then, abruptly, she felt a canteen at her lips, and Pascual was saying, "Drink, drink a little."

She clutched at the canteen, almost knocking it from his hand. She gulped two long swallows before he snatched it away.

She heard Fannin swear, heard him say, "Don't spill it, you bitch!"

"We got to stop now," Pascual said.

"How much farther?" Fannin said.

"Maybe ten miles."

"Ain't you ever sure of anything?"

"It been while back since I been there," Pascual said.

Fannin said, "It better not be no farther. I been giving my water to the girl, and I got only a swallow left."

She thought, *He's lying. Only once did he give me a drink. Or was it twice? He's been sneaking drinks for himself.*

"How much you got left, Injun?" Fannin said.

"I give her most of mine."

"How much, I said."

"Maybe enough," the Quechan said. "But we don't drink until morning."

They overslept, after a fitful night tortured by thirst. The rising sun was already above the mountain range, and burning as it touched them.

They had been without food since breakfast of the day before yesterday, the day of the breakout.

She was weak from lack of food, but she had no hunger.

There was only thirst.

Fannin drank from his canteen while she covertly watched. He drank deeply, she thought, and that enraged her.

He saw her watching, and lifted the canteen and shook it and there was no sound.

"Empty," he said.

"Pig!"

"Lady," he said, "I gave you four, five drinks yesterday. You forgetting?"

Suddenly she was in doubt. *Was* she forgetting? She remembered only one. Or was it two? It might have been more. She could not be sure. She felt a twinge of shame that she might be falsely accusing him. She dropped her eyes from his.

Then Pascual was offering his canteen, and she drank from it. From the heft of it she knew there was no more than a drink or two in it.

And many miles yet to go.

She handed it back to him, and he took only a mouthful before recapping it.

He turned away then and once again led the way.

She wondered if she could make it.

And, again, she thought, *Oh, God! May there be water when— if—we get there.*

The sun reached its zenith, and still the mountains seemed beyond their reach.

And then, suddenly it seemed, they were at the base of the range that rose steeply from the floor of the desert.

We made it! she thought, and tried to cry out the words, but they would not come.

"Where?" Fannin said. *"Tinajas?"* His voice was no more than a croak.

Pascual did not answer.

"Where?" Fannin said again.

The Quechan had been sucking on a pebble for a long time. Now he spit it out.

"Up there," he said, and jerked his head at the side of the mountain.

"How far?"

"Maybe third way, maybe quarter."

Fannin said, "Get at it."

They began the climb. There was a trail here, worn over the years. But it was steep, too steep almost. They gasped for breath, forcing their way on because they knew they would die if they didn't.

And then they reached the first of the tanks, saw the jutting rim of the cavity in the granite rock of the mountainside.

She saw no bones, and that gave her hope.

They clawed their way up to the rim.

And stared down into the dry, sunbaked granite hole.

"Empty!" Fannin said, outraged.

She began to cry, dry sobs racking her body. A cry without tears. To have tears, you needed water.

"How many tanks are there?" Fannin said.

"Six, eight," Pascual said. "But they high up them rock wall."

"Maybe they got water in them. Climb up there and see."

Pascual studied the cliff behind the tank, then shrugged. Fannin and Opal watched as he clambered up it.

A long time later he came sliding down.

"They dry too," he said.

Fannin gave him a bitter look. "You had to lead us here!"

A parody of a childhood prayer came to Opal's mind: *Now I lay me down to die.*

She glanced at the men, and knew this was the end. Even Pascual was beaten.

There was a growth of mesquite nearby, among the surrounding boulders.

Pascual sought its meager shade and lay down. She could see in his face that he, too, had given up. He sprawled out and closed his eyes.

Now, she thought, *he lays him down to die.*

She knew then that it was the end for all of them.

They lay inert, lifeless, and the hideous birds from hell, the vultures, came to circle over them.

It was the crash of thunder that awakened her.

She tried to call out to the others, but she couldn't.

But they were already awake.

She stared at the sky, and the vultures were gone. So was the sun. Now her sight was filled with an army of storm clouds marching up from the south.

Up from the Sea of Cortez, she thought, recalling the thin cloud streak on the horizon the previous day.

She forced the cry from her parched throat; "Will it rain?"

Pascual said, "Maybe. Maybe dry storm."

"It's a thunderstorm! Didn't you hear it?"

"I heard," he said. "We get thunder. But maybe it dump rain some other place."

"Maybe, maybe," Fannin said. "You want good news, don't ask an Injun."

His comment, too, angered her. "So! What's your answer?"

"It'll rain," he said.

And, almost with his words, it came.

It came with another crash of thunder and a bolt of lightning that struck the mountain above them.

A cloudburst followed.

They did not move.

Not at first.

They simply opened their mouths to the torrent and tried to drink it in.

But, of course, they couldn't. Not enough to do more than tantalize their terrible thirsts.

Soon they sat up and stared at the water cascading down the fissures of the granite wall, and they could hear the gurgle of it as the bottom of the basin began to fill.

They crawled to the edge then, tempted to risk injury on the slippery smooth boulders that surrounded it.

Opal had a wild impulse to throw herself down into the still, shallow pool.

Pascual grabbed her shoulder.

"No good," he said. "You wait. I get canteens and I fill."

Presently he was climbing down the wet-slick granite.

He filled the canteens, then clambered up to where Fannin reached down to grab his hand to help him out. Once out, Fannin dropped his hand quickly. A sign of how he felt about Indians, Opal thought.

Pascual handed one canteen to Opal. She took it readily and put it to her lips.

"Drink slow," the Quechan said.

He still held the other canteen.

Fannin eyed it, then his glance moved to Pascual's face.

Pascual appeared to smile faintly, then uncorked the canteen. He drank from it before handing it to Fannin.

Fannin took it. Still staring at Pascual, he deliberately wiped the canteen spout with his hand before he raised it to his own mouth.

CHAPTER 5

TOO soon, the storm moved on.

It left only a few inches of water on the bottom of the *tinajas.* But there was enough for them to drink their fill and to replenish the canteens.

And enough to draw animals from out of nowhere, creatures almost as thirsty as themselves. Such as a small band of the wild, vicious *javelinas,* boarlike beasts, all bristles and tusks.

They were small, but with those tusks they could rip a man's leg to ribbons.

They could survive, when necessary, on cholla and prickly-pear cactus when found, getting moisture and food both from the pads, blunting the spines with leather-tough mouths.

It was Pascual who first heard them coming. Wise in the way of the desert, he had earlier found a broken mesquite limb and had it near him as he lay recuperating between drinks from the newly filled canteens.

With the quenching of their thirst, hunger moved upon them.

"By God," Fannin said, "I'm hungry enough to eat dog meat!"

"No dogs out here," Pascual said.

"Don't get smart with me, Injun."

"You eat coyote, maybe?" Pascual said.

"I said, don't get smart."

The Quechan picked up the mesquite limb.

"Put that damn club down!"

"You don't hear?" Pascual said. *"Javelina* come."

Fannin listened.

From somewhere nearby, there was the sound of small hooves striking against the rocky terrain. It was followed by a wild mix of snorts and snuffles, and then a half-dozen of the nearsighted animals appeared at the opposite rim of the *tinaja*.

Without hesitation they went skidding down into the basin, accompanied by squeals and grunts.

"Pork," Pascual said. He stood up, club in hand, staring at them but making no move.

"Well," Fannin said, "you going to throw that club or not?"

"No kill that way," the Quechan said. But still he hesitated.

"Go on!" Fannin said.

Abruptly, Pascual slipped into the tank,. club held at the ready. The nearest *javelina* raised up from drinking, turned abruptly and charged at him, stinking up the air behind it from its musk gland.

Pascual jumped aside and smashed down with his club. He caught the beast across the spine, breaking it.

The *javelina* squealed its agony, threshed wildly, then crawled with its hind quarters dragging, lunging with its bared tusks, trying to the last to slash him.

Pascual swung again and again at the tough little boar. Slowly he clubbed it to death.

Opal, watching from the rim, said, "Oh, my God! Stop!"

Fannin grinned. "You like pork, girl?"

She cried to Pascual, "Look out!"

Another of the *javelinas*, likely the clubbed one's mate, had lifted its head from the water. It turned and made a rush for Pascual. He jumped aside. The animal rushed on by and kept going, clambering its way up out of the hole.

Then, always eccentric, the others abruptly followed the one, and they disappeared as quickly as they had arrived.

"Crazy bastards," Fannin said. "You never know what they'll do next." He paused, looking at Opal. "I'll say this for the Injun, it took guts to go down there amongst them."

Pascual was climbing out, dragging the carcass with him.

Fannin reached down and lifted it.

Pascual said, "You got matches?"

"Lucky so," Fannin said. "I'd hate to try to chew that tough little bastard in the raw."

It took a while to even partly roast the chunks that Fannin worried from the carcass with a pocketknife.

In the end they did chew the flesh half raw.

"Best pork I ever ate," Fannin said.

Opal didn't dispute that.

And after the meal, they slept. And slept.

She awoke as first light was beginning to show above an escarpment.

She lay still, turning only her head as she peered about, trying to pierce the final gloom of the night.

Then she heard the sound of a creaking pack rig and the stomp of approaching hooves. And the sudden off-key bray of a burro.

She did not move. *They've caught us,* she thought. *All the agony of these past days has gone for nothing. Back to that hellish cell on Prison Hill. I'd rather die.*

Then, angrily, she sat erect as the pack animal moved past her a few yards away, heading for the rim of the *tinaja.*

And across its withers, ahead of a meager pack, a scarecrow figure of a man hung facedown.

By now, both men were awake and staring too.

Fannin jumped to his feet, strode fast to catch the burro, stopping it as it reached the verge of the basin.

"Give me a hand," he said as Pascual moved to his side.

Together they dragged the man free. The burro moved on and stopped at the brink of the *tinaja.* They laid the man out.

"Bring a canteen," Fannin called to Opal.

He took it from her, and as Pascual held up the man's

head, he tipped the water so that a dribble went into the open mouth.

There was a faint groan after a troubled swallow. Then nothing.

"Old bastard is near dead," Fannin said. "Those white whiskers make him look like a dried-up prickly pear."

"Prospector," Pascual said.

"For sure."

"What could he find out here?" Opal said. "Is there gold?"

"It don't have to be here to bring out his kind. All it takes is to believe it's here," Fannin said. "But he may be the only one of his kind in this whole damn desert."

"Will he live?" she said.

"I doubt it. He must be eighty if he's a day. And God knows how long without water. I noticed them water bags on his pack was deflated empty."

Fannin tried to give the desert rat another drink, but this time there was no swallow.

Pascual laid the head back. "He gone," he said.

"He come close to making it," Fannin said. "Must have threw himself over the burro and hoped it'd find water."

"Which it did," Opal said.

At that moment, as if knowing he was being discussed, the animal turned away from the basin and looked back at them.

"You can trust a jack to know where he can't climb," Fannin said. "Even thirsty as he is."

Nobody spoke for a moment, the burro standing there watching them. Then Pascual poured water into his hat and took it to him.

Fannin said, "Let's see what's left in that pack." He approached the animal, which remained quiet, and unlashed the load hitch.

But first he withdrew from it a Winchester rifle with a battered stock. He checked the magazine and found it partly loaded. He laid it close by, without comment, and turned his attention to the pack.

There was a dozen cans of food.

And two empty canvas water bags. He handed them to Pascual. "Big luck, getting these. Fill them."

Pascual did not move. "The rifle is loaded, eh?"

Fannin glanced at him but did not answer.

"I ask you question," Pascual said.

"You saw me check it," Fannin said then.

There was a long stare between them, neither speaking. Then the Quechan turned away and went down into the *tinaja* with the empty bags.

Conley was almost out of water as he neared the vicinity of the *tinajas*.

He approached cautiously, considering that the convicts were likely to be holed up there. Their tracks were partly obliterated by the downpour, but he was certain the tanks had been their destination.

For a long spell, he remained below, studying the higher terrain. Finally he decided to move on. The guards with whom he'd spoken back at the prison had said there were no weapons unaccounted for, indicating the prisoners had escaped unarmed.

Thus, he began the ascent with some confidence, leading his horse and the pack mule.

He was hoping, for the sake of the girl as well as his own, that there was water up there.

As far as arresting them, that was a familiar part of his job, for which he had only a routine anxiety. That's assuming, of course, they were without weapons.

They had got the pack together again on the burro, with the water bags and their canteens, and had drunk fully from the water hole.

Pascual said, "We go southeast pretty soon now. Is trail take us deep in Mexico."

"Like hell!" Fannin said. "I got business east along the border at Sonoita."

"Too far," the Quechan said. "Is water at place call Tinajas of Papagos in Mexico."

"Dammit! I don't want to go down there."

"I do," Pascual said. "I got enough white-man law for me."

"The girl and me," Fannin said, "we're going to Sonoita. It's a border town I know. Right on the Arizona border."

"Mexico better for me," Pascual said. "Better for Opal, too." He paused. "Why I listen to you?"

"One big reason is I got the rifle. And I'm taking the girl with me."

Opal said, "Why?"

Fannin grinned. "Maybe I want to get better acquainted. And I got the mule and supplies." He slapped his hand against the breech of the rifle he was holding. "This says so."

She was silent.

"You go with the Injun, here, you go without food or drink." He paused. "Your choice, girl."

What choice did she have? she thought. She looked at Pascual. His face was without expression.

"I'll have to go with him, Pascual. I can't go through again what we've just been through. I mean, no water, no food. You understand?"

Fannin said, "I do believe this girl has fell in love with me. So you go your way, Injun, and me and her will go mine."

Pascual shook his head. "She go with you, I go too."

Fannin was about to object, when suddenly the burro brayed. An answering bray came from the slopes below them.

"Sounds like company," Fannin said. He slipped over to the edge of a rocky shelf.

Pascual was close behind him. "What you see?"

Fannin stared down the escarpment. "Nothing yet."

"Maybe prison guards."

"Not likely. But it could be a posse."

"There! I see!" Pascual said in a low voice. "Coming up rocks. Maybe two hundred yards."

"Yeah, I see the bastard," Fannin said. "And, by God, I recognize him. Seen him around Casa Grande a time or two."

"Who he is?"

"U.S. marshal. Name of Connery, something like that."

The first bullet went past Conley's shoulder and struck the horse. It reared, jerking the reins loose from Conley's grasp, then collapsed to lie still as he threw himself behind a cover of boulders.

The pack mule, its lead tied to the horse's saddle, pulled in panic, breaking away to disappear into the surrounding brush.

Conley swore, hearing it go, but keeping his eyes above, searching for sight of his attacker.

If it's them, they got a rifle somewhere, he thought. *And that makes the job a hell of a lot tougher.* He didn't let his mind dwell on the dead horse and runaway pack animal. *First things first,* he thought.

He had to close in on his assailant or assailants, whoever they were. He was almost certain they were the convicts. Why would anyone else out here have reason to attack him?

It would be a risky climb, and he lay in concealment, gathering a will to move. Seeing no one above, he jumped to his feet and made a long run to another cluster of rocks. And heard two shots smack and ricochet to either side of him.

Too close, he thought. *Too damn close.*

Too late, he found his cover was poor as another slug slammed into the earth beside him. It was suicide to stay there, and he was up again and running for another outcrop of granite.

Three more shots came before he reached his goal, and

the last one tore a chunk from the heel of his right boot, causing him to trip and fall on his final step.

He went down just short of his cover and sprawled helplessly, braced for a finishing shot to come.

From the ledge, Pascual saw this and said, "Shoot quick!"

Fannin had cocked the Winchester. He took quick aim and pressed the trigger. There was no fire, just a click.

He tried again. Same result.

"Out of cartridges," he said. "All that desert rat had in it."

"Was no more in pack?"

"You see any? I didn't."

"What we do now?"

"Run for it," Fannin said. "I killed his horse anyway. That'll slow him down some."

"Why you stupid and kill horse? We could use for girl."

"You damn fool, I was trying for the man."

"Lousy shot," the Quechan said.

Fannin's face hardened. "Anybody can miss once in a while." He paused. "With me it don't happen often. Something for you to remember, Injun."

Opal had come over to them. "Who is it?"

"U.S. marshal," Fannin said. "Name of Connery."

"Connery?" she said. "Not Conley?"

"That's it. Conley, You know him?"

"He's the one took me in."

"Looks like he's trying again," Fannin said. "We better get some distance on him while we can."

"He waste all bullets," Pascual said. "Only kill horse."

Opal felt a startling relief. She tried not to let it show on her face. She said, "We better move on quick."

"My intentions, girl," Fannin said.

They had just started off when Conley's pack mule appeared, heading directly for the tank water.

"This must be our lucky day," Fannin said. "Grab him before he breaks a leg trying to get into that tank."

Pascual grabbed the trailing lead rope and fought the animal as it tried to move on.

They lost a few minutes but finally overcame its stubbornness.

"Hurry!" Opal said. She had an anxious look.

They moved off fast down the other side of the escarpment. Pascual still had some struggle with Conley's pack animal.

Fannin said, "Dammit, Injun, can't you handle that mule?"

"Is marshal's mule. And you shoot his horse. Why you worry? You think he catch up?"

"I don't know. I think I might have shot him in the foot, the way he went down, but I ain't sure. I hope to hell so. Keep moving. He was wearing a gun belt and handgun and carrying a rifle."

"Oh, God," Opal said. "I don't want him to catch me again!"

"Who the hell does?" Fannin said. "Move fast, move fast!"

"I wish we could have filled his empty canteens," she said.

"Well, we got ours, and the desert rat's water bags too, and that's a hell of a lot more than he's got. I figure we get out of rifle range, he'll have to drop back to the tanks to drink, and we'll build up more lead on him."

"I hope so," Opal said. "I hope so."

As they got moving, Fannin said to her, "Something bothers me, girl. Something don't set quite right. You sounded relieved I wasn't able to kill that marshal."

"I don't like to see anybody killed," she said.

He was silent for a long time. Then he said, "Well, I can understand that. I never been a bloodthirsty bastard myself. But killing him would have got him off our trail for good. And it'd be too late for anybody else to run us down." He paused. "You can see that, can't you?"

"Yes, I can see it."

"You got to make up your mind how far you'll go to keep from going back to the lockup. You got to decide if you want more than anything to be free. I'm saying this now because there may be another showdown up ahead, and I want to know if I can trust you."

When she didn't answer, he said, "Well? Can I?"

"I don't want to go back any more than you do."

"That ain't what I asked."

"What did you ask?"

"I'm asking if you're willing to pay the price to stay out of that hellhole."

"I'm willing."

"Any price?"

"Any price within reason," she said.

"Dammit! That ain't any answer at all."

"It's the only answer I can give you," she said.

Conley had crawled to cover after a moment of playing possum.

He was surprised when no further shots came after the first few.

For a while he lay pondering this. Then gradually he began to wonder if his attackers—he still assumed they were the convicts—had resumed their flight. Since they were armed, he could think of no reason for their moving on without killing him first.

Eventually he figured he had to find out, and again he began a cautious climb toward the *tinajas*.

When he reached there, the fresh tracks of the two men, the girl, and the animals, and the body of the old prospector soon told him the story.

He swore violently as he found the half-dozen ejected shells, and guessed his attacker had run out of ammunition. He had let them get away, and now they had two pack animals, water, and provisions. And he had none.

He cursed again as he limped his way down into the tinaja to drink. Limped because of a boot heel half shot away, one hell of a handicap for a man crossing the desert on foot.

CHAPTER 6

THE heat was even worse. The air shimmered.

But now they had the pack animals, a few provisions, and water.

"Too bad you killed the horse," Opal said.

"You going to complain?" Fannin said. "Just like a woman!"

"I just wish we had something to ride. We could have spelled off on it."

"Well, we don't, so forget it."

She hated his way of speaking, but she had a need to talk. Pascual was up ahead, leading one pack animal. She followed, with Fannin just behind her with the other.

She said, "The marshal, do you think he won't give up?"

"I know it. His kind are stubborn bastards."

"Maybe he'll die. I mean without a way to carry water."

There was something close to concern in the way she said it.

"I hope so," Fannin said.

"He visited me once while I was in jail, before the trial," she said.

"So?"

"I think he regretted arresting me."

"Yeah? So why is he trailing you now?"

"Maybe it's you he wants."

"Don't fool yourself, lady. You're the one he's really after. I'm small potatoes compared to you. I remember those stories about you in the newspapers. Hell, you got more coverage than the shoot-out at the OK Corral. If he could bring you in again, he'd get the kind of fame could put him into politics."

Politics? The idea startled her. From what she remembered of him, he'd not be a man with ambitions like that. He had just been a man who did a job he'd sworn to do, regardless of consequences. A man who'd shown some sympathy for her plight.

That's why the thought of his dying on the desert could cause her concern.

But, she thought, *I would die myself if he brought me back to that hellhole of a prison.*

Conley drank his fill from the tank. Once satisfied, he climbed out and rested on the rim.

If only he had a way to carry water. He cast about him, hoping, and found nothing. His glance rested on the dead prospector.

The buzzards were circling overhead, waiting for him, Conley, to leave. He swore at them, wondering grimly if he might himself provide their next meal.

For a moment, he considered trying to cover the old man's corpse with rocks to protect it. He rejected the idea at once.

He had to get on the trail again. His quarries already had a lead.

He stood up, and came close to tumbling back into the *tinaja.*

Damned shot-off boot heel, he thought.

He sat down again, took out a pocketknife, and cut at the leather until he had smoothed it off. He then hacked off the opposite heel to match. When he stood again, he felt himself balanced, although the lowered heels would take some getting used to.

Riding boots were never meant for walking anyway,. he thought.

He stared once more at the prospector's body, and again at the vultures wheeling above. Then he turned to follow the tracks of those he pursued.

It was tough going. The unaccustomed walking, complicated by the altered boot heels, soon caused his calves to cramp. He had to repeatedly halt for relief, and finally stopped before sundown, unable to go on, the muscle cramps aggravated by dehydration.

It irritated him that he had to quit because the tracks were easy to see. They had led down to the old *camino,* and he took out his pocket map to discover the trail led east, just south of the border, eventually reaching the Mexican town of Sonoita.

All he had to do was follow the trace, and here he was, stymied by a fool thing like leg muscles that knotted up.

He resigned himself to sleep, finally, and awoke sometime after midnight. There was a quarter moon, and he had a great thirst that kept him awake. After a bit, he arose and studied the old trace, wondering if there was enough light to follow it.

And enough light to spot the rattlers, sure to be out now.

He decided to take the chance.

And almost at once he nearly stepped on one.

He caught the movement just in front of his left boot as he put it down. He jumped back, the hair on his neck prickling, as a sidewinder slithered across his path.

He stood transfixed, swearing until his nerves calmed down.

Then he set off again, eyes wide open to pierce the shadows cast here by the creosote and brittlebush. He walked until dawn, and saw only two more of the reptiles, but each one gave him a start.

His leg cramps were coming back, and he halted. His thirst had grown, but there was nothing he could do about that. Carefully, he checked out a clump of greasewood and lay down in the early morning shade of it to rest.

He dozed off, for how long he could not tell, because the sun had become obscured by the time the wind and the bite of the blowing sand awakened him.

When the sandstorm began, Pascual said, "It go to get bad. We stop now."

"Like hell," Fannin said. "Not with that damn marshal legging after us."

"He be smart, he stop too," Pascual said.

"Yeah? Well, maybe he ain't that smart. Or maybe he's law-dog stubborn enough to keep on, regardless of his smarts. I been on the run from more like him than you ever have, I'm thinking. And I figure him to be one that hates to let go."

"Trail hard to see."

"By God, we'll keep on until we can't see it at all," Fannin said.

The Quechan studied him for a moment, squinting against the stinging sand. Then suddenly he nodded. "You the boss, white man," he said.

"And you damn well better believe it, Injun."

Pascual resumed the lead into the thickening dust. Once, as they trudged through a spot that felt powdery under their feet, he halted as if undecided of his direction, then moved quickly on.

"I thought he was lost there for a minute," Fannin said, moving close to Opal and raising his voice close to her ear.

She gave no sign she had understood.

He shrugged and moved away.

She tried to keep her sight on Pascual's tall form, staying as close to the pack mule he led as she safely could.

It was foolish to keep on, she thought. Pascual had been right. Even he could get lost in this poor visibility.

The sting of sand against her face was almost blinding, and she wondered why he did protest now against pressing on.

Did he feel that dominated by Fannin? She had thought he was stronger than that. Somehow, she still thought so.

The time came, finally, when the sandstorm grew so strong that the animal he led came to a halt. Hooves planted, it refused to go on.

Fannin, close behind Opal, bumped into her, nearly knocking her down. He cursed and yelled against the wind at Pascual, but only she could catch the words.

"What's wrong?"

And then they saw the man on horseback facing them, directly ahead. He wore range clothing, with a drover's hat held by tie strings under his chin. A neckerchief covered his mouth and nostrils. His mount was a buckskin, a color hard to see through the dust.

Words passed between the rider and Pascual, words neither Opal nor Fannin could hear.

Pascual turned then and shouted, "We stop!"

Almost as he spoke, surprisingly the wind began to lessen, dropping its sting, though the dust stayed thick in the air.

The mounted man pulled down his neckerchief and stared beyond Pascual and the mule and Opal. He held his eyes on Fannin.

Fannin stared back. His stare grew hard.

The horseman spoke then, projecting his voice to carry. "That you, Fannin?"

Fannin did not answer at once. Then he said, "Yeah."

"Don't you recognize a friend?"

"I recognize you, Kuster."

"Sure you do, Sam. Been a while."

"Maybe not long enough, Mike."

"You ain't holding hard feelings, are you, Sam?"

"Damn right I am."

"Why, Sam, that's a shame. Everything can be explained."

"Yeah?"

"Got any water?"

"No."

"The hell you say. Why, Sam, I can see a couple of water bags hanging on that burro right there." He paused. "I recall I bought the last drink between us. Tequila, that time. I'll settle now for water."

Fannin's eyes focused on the revolver, holstered on Kuster's hip. He showed a thoughtful look.

"All right," he said. "Light and get your drink."

"I knew you wouldn't refuse an old pardner," Kuster said.

He dismounted and strode to the burro's side and unhooked a water bag. He drank deeply from it.

"Man can get mighty dry crossing this desert," he said then.

Fannin had stepped close to the horse, studying the brand on its haunch.

"Been in the south, I see," he said. "Ain't that one of old Don Luis Quijada's horses?"

Opal studied Kuster as he gave his answer. Same young hardcase type as Fannin, she judged. Lighter hair, but lean, with a similar build. Even his grin now had a resemblance to Sam's.

"My own got shot during a banking transaction that went sour down Hermosillo way. Seen this one hitched out front of the bank I was trying to make a withdrawal from. Old Don Luis's own, maybe, just like he owns the bank. Ain't that a coincidence?"

"You taken now to robbing greaser banks?" Fannin said.

"Looked easy," Kuster said. "And I figured it a step up from rustling cows."

"Not your stomping grounds down there," Fannin said.

"No. And I don't figure on going back. Maybe you and me, we can team up again farther east, like old times."

"Ain't likely."

Kuster drank again, recorked the canvas bag. "Your choice," he said. He swept his glance over Pascual and let it linger on Opal. "Ain't those prison clothes I'm seeing? Yuma pen, maybe?"

Fannin said nothing.

"Sure as hell," Kuster said, still looking at her. "Where was you and your friends headed?"

Fannin hesitated, then said, "Sonoita."

"Sonoita? Friend Sam, you must have lost your way for sure during this dust blow. This trail we're on is the one from them old Papago water holes. Where I got my last drink."

Fannin's face grew hard. He turned to Pascual. "You son of a bitch! You done it on purpose."

The Quechan showed nothing, just returned his stare.

Kuster laughed. "Hell, Sam, ain't you learned not to trust an Injun?"

"Got lost," Pascual said.

"The hell you did! You went the way you wanted to go."

Kuster said, still grinning, "You ought to shoot the bastard."

"Lend me your gun," Fannin said.

Kuster laughed again. "No, Sam, I don't reckon I'll do that. I ain't quite sure yet that you don't hold me a grudge. I hope it ain't so though."

His glance went to the rifle shoved under the burro's pack lashings. He took hold of its stock and jerked it loose, levered it, and pointed it off to one side. He triggered it then, and heard only the hammer striking the firing pin.

"Empty, eh, Sam? Wondered why you asked to borrow my handgun."

Fannin looked over at Pascual, as if weighing him as a possible ally against this hardcase former associate.

Kuster saw this, and said, "You want me to kill him for you, Sam?"

Fannin said quickly, "No. He still knows his way around this damn desert better than we do. I just got to make him mind what I tell him."

"Whatever you say, Sam. Maybe I can help you do that."

A sharp gust of wind struck them as he spoke.

"More storm come," Pascual said.

Another gust came, and another, and then the steadily increasing blow began. The sand and dust rose again in the still, murky air. It thickened fast, until the light diminished to that of dusk.

"We wait," Pascual said.

"The bastard's right," Kuster said. "No use fighting this no more. Not when you got food and water."

But the sand blast was too great now to dig into the scant food packs.

They tied the animals to the bushes, and huddled in the brush themselves.

The dust storm grew in violence until it was worse than it had been before.

They lay there together, sharing misery, eyes closed, faces protected by their arms.

Conley had come to where the trace to the south forked off from the trace to Sonoita. He reached it during the lull after the first blow.

Which way did they go? He pulled out his map again.

There was a trace showing southeasterly into Mexico. It ended in an undesignated dot, this being outside the confines of Arizona. Could the dot be the location of the old Tinajas of the Papagos, he wondered? He swore a little then at the prison superintendent who had given him the Arizona map and sent him off on a chase into Mexico. Well, the blame was on himself for not being better prepared. Too much short notice, he supposed. Not that *that* was an excuse, either.

He spent some time carefully scrutinizing the forks.

There were no tracks after the blow.

But then, as he was about to give up the search and return to the Sonoita trace, he saw a can lying half buried in a drift of sand.

He picked it up and studied it. The label was unweathered, the printing on it unfaded: "McGuffey's Peaches."

He thought it could be one of the cans from his own pack mule. If so, they *had* taken the trail south.

While he considered this, he drove the blade of his pocketknife into the can top and got it open, and drank the nectar that was too quickly gone.

He used the blade then to bring out the juicy chunks.

It helped his thirst, brought sudden hunger.

He ignored this, got to his feet, and began trudging again. God, he had to catch up to them. He had to catch up and *capture* them. If for no other reason than he had to eat.

And then he felt the first stirrings of the wind again.

He knew the dust storm was about to renew itself.

He could not let that stop him now. He'd continue on, no matter what.

It blew from the southwest, continuously blasting his right side, veering him to the left, so that every few paces he had to make certain he was still on the trace. This became ever more difficult, as his exhaustion grew and his senses dulled with fatigue. Three times he found he had wandered off the trail, and spent anxious periods before he found it again.

He couldn't let himself get lost now.

This time, the storm lasted for hours, or so it seemed. Still he kept on, though frequently now he had to stop to rest.

Had those he pursued kept on? he wondered. Why should they, if they believed he would have stopped? The thought gave him hope.

If they had halted, he was gaining on them with every step. He held that foremost in his mind. It was all that kept him going.

From time to time, Pascual or Fannin or Kuster raised his head from where they huddled, eyes slitted against the blowing sand, to give a sweeping glance at the tethered animals.

It was Kuster who suddenly sat up, cursing.

He reached over and grabbed Fannin's shoulder and tugged.

Fannin ignored the grasp at first.

The tugging became a series of jerks. It finally aroused Fannin from an exhausted stupor. He sat up, swearing himself.

"What the hell?"

"The buckskin is gone," Kuster shouted against the wind.

"What?"

"My horse. It's broke loose. Wandered off."

"What the hell you want me to do about it?" Fannin shouted back. He lay down again.

Kuster got to his feet, staggered for a moment as he strove for balance against the gale. He forced his way over to where the buckskin had been tied. He came back then, still swearing to himself.

The horse was gone, and that was it. Until this miserable dust storm was over.

Conley kept on. Occasionally, he was still stopped by leg cramps caused by the altered boots. But the pain was not as severe as it had been the previous day.

Getting toughened up to walking, he thought. Always a problem for a riding man.

The big problem was the ever-blasting sand. The side of his face was raw from it. When he touched fingers to his jowl, they came away moist with blood.

Step by painful step, he went on, mindless now, having found a refuge in stupor.

The appearance of the buckskin horse startled him. It seemed to startle the horse, too.

For a long moment each stood unmoving, eyes on the other. Then Conley's fell to the trailing reins.

He began talking, soft talk as he slowly approached the nervous animal, and then he realized what he was saying could not be heard over the fury of the wind.

But he continued his easy approach, fighting his urge to close in fast.

It was a God-given chance, and he could not afford to muff it. Strangely, the horse remained still.

Still until he reached for the loose reins thrashing in the wind.

As he made a frantic grab for them, the buckskin shied away and disappeared, obscured at once in the dust-shrouded greasewood.

His chance was gone. He stood as if transfixed, stunned by disappointment. Hopeless. Cursing.

And the horse came back into sight, hesitated, then came close, as if seeking comfort in the presence of man.

Conley acted by instinct this time, diving for the reins, catching them and holding them with an iron grip as the mount fought the bit.

Abruptly then, it lost all fight. A fine-looking gelding, Conley thought, judging by what he could see through squinted eyes. Somebody's favorite saddle mount, maybe. Owner a person of means, judging by the expensive Mexican saddle. Some *hacendado,* maybe.

But what was it doing up here in the desert, a hundred miles or more north of the nearest *hacienda?*

Broke loose in the windstorm, probably. But from where, and from who?

No matter what, he thought. He now had a mount, and would walk no more.

He swung up into the saddle, seating quickly as the horse, skittish in the wind, bucked a couple of times before settling down.

But he could not force it against the tangent of the wind. It refused to fight the driving sand, and Conley's spurless heels driven into its flanks would not force it.

He gave up finally, dismounted, and tethered it, the thought coming to him that if those he pursued were still on foot, he would overtake them, now that he had a mount. And, God knew, he could use a rest himself.

The wind had stopped again.

Conley awoke from a troubled doze. His first thought was of the horse. He shot a glance to where he had tethered it. It was still tied, head lowered, rump to the direction from which the wind had blown.

It had been ridden hard, he judged by closer scrutiny. As if by a rider on the dodge. For a moment he wondered how much he could get out of it. Enough, he hoped. He'd not have to work it hard now to close the gap between himself and the convicts. That's if they were still walking.

He was pretty certain they would be—it wasn't likely there'd be many horses roaming loose around the desert.

He mounted. This time the gelding submitted passively, and he headed it into the trace, more difficult than ever to pick out now. After a while he found the horse seemed able to do this better than he, and he gave it its head, although he kept alert to see it did not wander.

And alert, too, that he did not blunder unexpectedly into a convict trio encampment. Even if they were again without firepower, as he judged by the evidence of the ejected shells and their quick departure at the Altas Tanks, he wanted to take them by surprise.

Two men against one, it paid to be careful. Two men and a woman, he thought. She could be as desperate as her companions.

Thinking back to those cells he'd seen dug into the caliche clay of Prison Hill, he put himself in her place and thought, *By God! I'd be desperate too.*

A squad of Rurales, the dreaded Rural Police of the dictator, Porfirio Diaz's Mexico, had lost the trail they had been following for days. The trail of a gringo bandit who had tried to rob a bank owned by the politically influential rancher, Don Luis Quijada, in Hermosillo.

A gringo who, when the attempt was thwarted, added further insult to the Don by stealing his favorite horse from in front of the bank, while Quijada was across the street in a cantina.

A horse on which he had made a getaway.

It was evidence of Don Luis's political clout that his request for a trio of Rurales to pursue the outrageous *gabacho* was immediately granted.

It was Don Luis's kind who kept Dìaz in power.

Now, as the second assault of the sandstorm faded, the three Rurales came out from under their covering ponchos. They were none the worse for wear.

Sandstorms were nothing to them. Nor were rebellious *peons*, or *bandidos* of any race, or anything else.

They roamed the deserts and the plains and the mountains of Mexico to administer hard justice to any or all whom they judged to be enemies of the state. Cossacks, they were called by many.

They were men on horseback with license to arrest, try, judge, sentence, and execute as they saw fit. They were chosen men, chosen for their temperament to enjoy these duties.

The sergeant, Razo, the tall, gaunt one with the aquiline nose and light skin, was the first now to speak.

"*Hombres,* we have lost time in our mission. Three of us, picked men all, chasing one gringo *bastardo* four hundred kilometers, and still he is on the loose. Think what this does to our reputations."

"We were close, *jefe,*" one of the Rurales said. "It was this cursed sand *chubasco* that spoiled our chance."

"And maybe he gets away for good," the other, who was named Chuy, said. He paused. "I am thinking, *jefe,* that all gringos look alike to me."

"Of course they do," Razo said. "But what do you mean?"

"I am thinking, if we can find a gringo, any gringo, we can take him back to Don Luis and say it is him."

"Don Luis is not easily fooled."

The first Rurale now said, "It is his pet horse, I think, that Don Luis wants most."

"Enough talk, *hombres,*" Razo said. "*Vàmonos!* We will find that *cabròn* of a gringo yet!"

As the wind dropped, the convicts and Mike Kuster debated their position.

"We'd have been halfway to Sonoita," Fannin said to Pascual, "if you hadn't led us on the wrong trail."

"Sonoita no good for me," the Quechan said. "Far down Mexico better."

"Not for me and Opal."

"For Opal, too."

"Like hell. Best for that girl is with me."

"You here too now," Pascual said.

"Don't smart-mouth me, Injun," Fannin said. He gave Pascual a raging look.

"You want fight?" Pascual said. "You got no bullets now."

Fannin's glance dropped over the big Quechan's physique. He said nothing.

Mike Kuster laughed. "He's a big 'un, ain't he, Sam? Too bad you don't want to be friends with me no more. I could help you out."

"He cost us a lot of water on this sidetrack," Fannin said. "I'm wondering if we got enough left to backtrack and reach Sonoita. How far is it to those Papago tanks?"

"Twenty miles, maybe. Didn't seem too far when I was riding. Walking is a different matter. Rough country. Worse than this. *Malpais* country with lava rock, some stretches. Take a look around you, Sam. We're entering the Pinacate area. Sierra Pinacate, the Mexicans call it."

Fannin, for the first time, tried to scan their surroundings. The air was still filled with dust.

"How the hell can I see anything?"

"You never been in the Pinacate before?"

"Not that I know of."

"Then you never been. It ain't a place you'd forget. Worst part of the desert. Called Sierra because it's strewn with old dead volcanos. Fields of lava spewed out a million years ago, maybe. You'll see them when it clears. Saguaros, ocotillo, ironwood, but dry, dry, dry. Except for them tanks. Ain't nobody lived here since the Sand Papagos left the *tinajas* years ago. Too much even for them, I reckon."

"How come you know all this?" Fannin said.

"Hell, I crossed part of it. And an old Mexican in Hermosillo told me about it, one night in a cantina."

"It looks like we've got to replenish our water at those Papago Tanks," Fannin said. "Damn this Injun's eyes!"

"Want me to get rid of him for you, Sam? We'd maybe have water enough then."

"I ain't that cold-blooded," Fannin said. "Not unless worse comes to worst."

"Looks like that prison life might have softened you up some, Sam. As I recall it, you never much cottoned to Injuns."

"Let's say he did me a favor or two while we were in there together."

"You don't talk friendly to him," Kuster said.

"You don't have to *like* a man to figure you owe him for a favor," Fannin said.

There was no favor: Fannin was using that as an excuse to deter Kuster from maybe shooting the guide. Fannin didn't like the trick Pascual had played on him, but he worried about being alone with an armed Kuster. There wasn't anything to prevent his onetime confederate from annihilating any of them if he got the urge.

Fannin kept remembering that Kuster had always been a little more erratic than most of their kind.

As witness the double cross back on that rustling venture.

I ever get that gun of his, Fannin thought, *I'll damn sure eliminate that worry.* He was wondering now if maybe he and Pascual together could overpower Kuster and get the weapon. Not likely, he thought. Kuster was pretty handy with a pistol. It would have to be by surprise.

Conley had been on the trail for a couple of hours before he picked up some blurred new tracks in the covering of drifts from the storm.

He wouldn't know if he was overtaking his quarries until he followed their sign for a while longer. He had been walking the buckskin, letting it have its head, aware of a need to save some reserve for what might be ahead.

After a time, though, urgency began to nag him. At a walking pace, he might just be holding even. Almost unconsciously he found he had put the horse into a trot. Once done, he held it there for a time.

When later he dropped it back to a walk, he judged it did not seem too worse for wear.

Thereafter he periodically put it to the faster pace. He had to catch up, he thought. He couldn't afford to ruin the tired mount, but he had to take some risk. It was a thin line on which he traveled.

Finally, though, he decided the horse could take no more, and he gave it its head at a slow walk that would gain nothing.

He must have dozed in the saddle, and was brought alert and erect as the buckskin nickered.

He halted, his skin crawling at the thought that the horse might have given him away.

A *malpais* area of dark basalt, vestige of an eons-ago volcanic eruption, hid what lay before him.

He dismounted at once, to make a lesser target.

He found a growth of ironwood and tied the buckskin's reins. A trail ahead laced through the *malpais,* a scant three feet wide. He entered it, carrying his rifle, cocked and ready, his Colt on his hip.

Three unarmed convicts, he thought. And one of them is a woman. But I better be on guard just the same.

It was the Indian who saw him first. The Indian was smart enough not to cry out. No telling what a sudden yell might do to a man with his finger on a Winchester trigger.

"Hold them high!"

Fannin and the girl saw him then. The three of them raised their hands.

Kuster, off in the malpais to relieve himself, heard the command. He jerked up his pants, grabbed his gun belt and buckled it, and made a cautious approach toward the voice.

In a moment he was peering through a fissure in the jumbled lava.

That must be the lawman they were running from, he thought.

He crouched there, his mind racing. The girl had revealed, and Fannin had admitted to him, that a U.S. marshal was on their trail. Kuster saw no badge, but no smart lawman tracking out here would be advertising his profession.

Kuster was fifty feet away. He put his hand on the butt of his six-gun, then drew it away. He could risk a shot from here, sure. But how fast could that marshal pivot and fire that saddle gun? And if either of them missed, a duel would follow, a duel through that splotch of *malpais,* and he, Kuster, with a handgun only, would be on the short end of it.

And what concern of his was it what happened to those three jailbirds?

None, he thought. He'd stay hid, watch and see what took place next. If only the girl or the damn fool Injun didn't let slip that he was with them. He trusted that Fannin wouldn't.

He wondered how the lawman had caught up, if he had never been in sight behind them. He wondered if he'd somehow got a horse.

Fannin, facing Conley, his hands in the air, was wondering how long it took that damn Kuster to relieve himself. Even if he hadn't heard the marshal's voice, he should be coming back by now.

The doubt hit him then. How could he rely on the two-timing bastard to come to their aid? Kuster looked out for Kuster, he ought to know that by now.

Fannin spoke up then. "You Conley?"

Conley nodded.

"How long we got to hold our hands like this? We ain't armed."

"We'll see."

"I can't hold them up much longer," Opal said.

Conley met her eyes. "All right, Opal. You can let yours down."

She gave him a grateful look.

Fannin didn't.

The Quechan watched without expression.

"It's a long way back to the prison," Conley said. "You can make it hard on yourselves, or you can make it some easy."

"What the hell does that mean?" Fannin said.

"Don't fight me, that's how."

"You know better."

"Yeah," Conley said. "I'm afraid so." He paused. "You found my stray pack mule, I see. Been eating high on the hog?"

None of them answered.

"Maybe you didn't dig deep enough in the pack," Conley said. "There's three pairs of manacles in there, loaned to me by the prison boss. That's what I meant by hard or easy."

Opal lost her grateful look. All three of them gave him a sullen stare.

"I can see now how it'll have to be," Conley said.

"You're a hard man, Marshal," Fannin said.

"Hard enough."

"We'll see," Fannin said. "I'm dropping my hands regardless. Shoot if you damn well please."

He dropped them to his sides.

The Quechan suddenly did the same.

"So," Fannin said. "Not hard enough to shoot an unarmed man."

"Don't bet too heavy on it."

Fannin gave him a long, appraising look. Some of the

cockiness went out of the outlaw's face. "Maybe so," he said. "Maybe so."

"Believe it," Conley said. "Opal, you are traveling with bad company."

"I've been close to worse this past year," she said.

"I suppose," he said.

He was studying the two male convicts. Take away those prison clothes, he thought, and you couldn't tell them from the men you saw every day on the street of any town.

That did not surprise him.

He had learned a long time ago that not many bad men ever looked the part.

CHAPTER 7

THE two men convicts walked awkwardly, their wrists manacled behind their backs.

After satisfying his thirst from their water supply, Conley had agreed they'd have to find the Papago tanks and refill the containers before starting a return trip.

The girl, light of weight, he let ride the buckskin, leading his pack mule. Seeing the silent pleading in her eyes, he had left her hands free, although he had his reservations about this.

He'd have to watch her closely, he thought. He was a fool to give her special treatment. His reasons went back to that remembrance of her unjust trial, and to all the other feelings he'd had about her ever since he'd brought her in that other time.

Fannin trudged in bitter silence, only occasionally bursting into a streak of swearing.

The Indian said nothing.

Conley said, "Keep moving."

"What the hell do you think we're doing?" Fannin said.

Fannin was the one to watch, Conley was thinking. A real hard case.

He glanced at Opal and frowned. She had a way of arousing a mixed feeling in him. The trouble was, he couldn't seem to keep her out of his mind.

Papago tanks was a flat complex of adjoining basins, spread in a nightmarish scene of eroded boulders and sharply fixed lava.

Even manacled, the male convicts did not hesitate to throw themselves to the water's edge to drink.

Conley held back to keep an eye on them as he helped the girl down from the saddle. The horse made for the water, beating her to it.

It was no time for being particular, Conley thought, watching the convicts and the horse share a pool.

There were floaters on the water surface, insects that came to drink and drown. The convicts shoved them aside with their faces.

Conley's own thirst drove him to the water. He lay prone next to Opal, keeping his holstered gun on the far side away from her, and drank as greedily as the others, but more briefly.

Temporarily satisfied, they sprawled a few feet from the tank, all of them now eyeing Conley.

It was Fannin who spoke first. "I heard of you, Marshal. Always get your man, they say. Like them police up in Canada they call the Mounties."

Conley made no comment.

"Did you see that damn prison before you took to tracking us? Ain't fit for an animal to live like that."

"Wages of sin," Conley said.

"Don't Bible-spout to me," Fannin said.

"Wasn't my intention."

"No, I reckon not. You don't look like a man who believes in much."

"I believe in the law," Conley said.

Fannin jerked his head toward Opal. "What kind of law is it that gives a girl like her five years in a cave? She was driv to it to save her mother from dying."

"I see you read the newspapers."

"She got a raw deal," Fannin said, "and you know it."

"What're you leading up to?"

"Nothing. Just stating a fact."

"I know the facts."

"Then treat her decent," Fannin said.

"She behaves, I will."

Opal stared at Fannin. His apparent sympathy for her seemed out of character.

"I didn't know you cared," she said.

"More than you know, girl," Fannin said. "You keep that in mind."

Conley was irritated by his words. Irritated more than he should be.

Fannin seemed to sense this, and looked amused. After a moment, he said, "It's a long trip back to that hell on a hilltop, Marshal. You up to watching us all the way?"

"Believe it."

"We'll see, we'll see," Fannin said.

Opal sensed a threat in his words. And why not, with his former confederate, Kuster, undoubtedly close by and watching.

Thinking of this, she was disturbed, rather than relieved. Kuster was one of the outlaw breed. Likely a killer.

What action might he take against the marshal?

And why should she care?

Was it because Conley had shown some regret after arresting her back there in Florence? She thought it was.

But against this was her terrible dread of confinement, the same dread that had driven her to escape in the company of two convicts in whom she had, at best, an uncertain trust.

She could not stand to go back.

But could she, either, stand to see Conley shot down in cold blood?

She'd had only one close experience with a man, the one with John Hartman, who disappointed her. A rambling, gambling, cold man who could not even consummate their marriage. It had left her vulnerable to men's minor attentiveness, even that reservedly expressed by the marshal.

Or that shown passively by Pascual . . . and hinted by Fannin, whose feelings she was almost certain were not sincere.

She judged now that this was a weakness in her, a dangerous one where Conley was concerned. A weakness she must steel herself against if she was to avoid return to the lockup. She did not owe him anything. If he had not arrested her in the first place, she wouldn't have ended behind bars.

And yet, she was torn by an irrational urge to warn him of the potential killer possibly lurking in the surrounding *malpais*.

She had to fight hard to suppress it.

She felt him appraising her but did not look up. She was afraid she would give something away.

Finally, though, she did raise her eyes.

He seemed about to speak, then changed his mind. He scowled, but the scowl did not seem to be for her. It was more like it was for himself.

Was he having doubts of his own? she wondered.

Then suddenly he did speak.

"Why?" he said.

"Why what?"

"Why did you break out?"

"To get free," she said. "What else?"

"Was it that bad?"

"I told you before the trial. I can't stand to be caged."

"And I told you, you should have thought of that."

"I should have thought of a lot of things . . . before I acted so foolish," she said.

"You realize that now."

"Of course I do!"

He did not speak for a moment, then he said, "Your mother, has she written you?"

"Her doctor did. She died of the lung disease."

"So what you attempted, all went for nothing."

"That made the confinement all the worse."

"Do you hate me?" he said.

"You had a job to do."

"Yes," he said. "And I have a job to do now."

"Why did you take it? I mean this job of hunting me down?"

"It wasn't my willing," he said. "I was ordered by some higher-ups."

"Once a lawdog, always a lawdog," Fannin said. "Tell the girl the truth, you get your kicks out of it. It's a game, ain't it?"

"Life is a game," Conley said. "We play the hands we're dealt."

Fannin's look lingered on him, then he said. "Well, we agree there. My sentiments exactly."

Kuster had followed them, dropping back to a distance when needed to cover himself in the sparse growth of desert flora, closing in as they reached the lava area around the Papago *tinajas*.

He had been shocked to see the marshal bring up the horse he had stolen from Don Luis Quijada. This after the convicts had been manacled back there in the basaltic badlands.

It had irritated him to see the girl riding his horse while he had to walk. His irritation grew as his thirst increased.

He was tempted, from time to time, to close in and take his chances with his handgun against the marshal. But the proper chance never seemed to come. More than once he cursed himself for not making a bushwhack try back there when he'd first seen the lawman.

It had been partly caused by the reputation of Conley, he realized now.

Well, by God, he wouldn't let that hold him back next time he had an opportunity!

The hard walking and his increasing thirst hardened his resolve on this.

And then, abruptly, his thought swung completely. He had no grudge against the marshal. And the marshal, to his knowledge, had no warrant outstanding for his arrest.

Why provoke a shoot-out? What was he to gain? He cared nothing for his three traveling companions, possibly excepting the girl.

All he wanted was one of the pack animals, and his horse, and to be free to head for Sonoita. Leave the marshal and his prisoners to their own problems.

Could he talk the lawman into this?

It might be worth the try. Hell, he'd even volunteer to help escort the convicts back to Yuma. That's it! Conley could damn sure use somebody when he needed sleep. There might even be some reward money coming if he helped.

He should have thought of this way back there in that strew of lava, he thought. Why stick his neck out shooting a lawman? Not for the likes of that Injun. Or Fannin, who held him a grudge. Or even for a roll in the sand with the girl.

He'd make friends with the marshal. He had his mind made up to do that now. That was the way to go.

He'd go on in where they loafed at the tanks. Cautiously, but with a big smile. Wasn't likely the lawman would shoot without provocation.

The more Kuster thought about it, the more confident he felt.

Opal saw Kuster approach, openly and smiling, keeping his hand well away from his holster.

From where Conley rested he could not see this.

Again she felt torn by her conflicting urges. One, to let Kuster come close and get the drop on the marshal. The other to cry out a warning that Kuster might kill him.

Something in her face must have alerted him. His body tensed, but he did not move. He was a fine-looking man, she thought.

It would be a shame to see him die.

And then her voice lashed out. "Look out! He'll kill you!"

He whirled, grabbed at his gun.

Her warning startled Kuster, too. Without thought, he jerked free his weapon.

He had it half raised when Conley's bullet caught him in the chest.

Kuster did not die at once. He lasted long enough to speak two sentences to Conley. One was, accusingly, "I was going to help you take them in." A long pause. Then, "Take care of that buckskin. Best damn horse I ever stole."

They all heard his words.

Pascual said nothing.

Fannin said, "The double-crossing son of a bitch! I might have known."

Opal looked suddenly ill.

So did Conley, as the dying man's words sank in. He turned a sick stare on her.

"A way to cut down the odds on me taking you in?" he said. "Is that why you hollered?"

"No!" The word was wrenched from her. "No! I thought he intended to kill you!"

He looked as if he wanted to believe her.

She turned away from him then and began to retch.

They had drunk, eaten what Conley rationed them, and slept. The convicts, Opal included, manacled and with ankles tied.

As dawn came, Conley was ready to start them on their way back.

That's when Fannin spoke up.

"Be best if you head for Sonoita and the border, Marshal."

"Best for you, maybe."

"Think about it," Fannin said. "There's a trail up from Sonoita clear to Gila Bend."

"A long trail," Conley said. He had out his map. "Hundred miles of desert, way I gauge it."

"Not near as rough as the way we come from Yuma. We can get water at Sonoita or Quitobaquito."

"And then?"

"Plenty of water at Ajo, halfway to Gila. I been that route, Marshal. I know what I'm saying."

"Sure you do. But is it true?"

"We get to Gila Bend, we could ride the good old Southern Pacific rail line back to the prison then. It'd sure beat the way we come."

"You got money for train fare?"

"Hell, the superintendent would damn sure wire fare money to bring us in."

"I'm thinking on it," Conley said.

"Like I said, I know the trail."

"That's the part that bothers me," Conley said.

"Look, I'm just wanting to make it easier for all of us. We go back the way we come, and maybe them *tinajas* at Altas are already dried up. Then what?"

The man had a point there, Conley thought.

Opal had told him the man he'd killed had once been a partner of Fannin's. Now he said to the rustler, "You want to cover up that body with rocks?"

Fannin said, "Hell no! Leave him for the coyotes and the buzzards. Me and him quit being friends some time ago."

"The buckskin was his horse," Conley said. "Got a fine Mexican saddle and a brand I'm not familiar with."

"Belongs to a rich *hacendado,* down Hermosillo way. Mex named Quijada. Kuster stole it from him."

"If this Kuster and you weren't friends, why was he traveling with you?"

"He stumbled in on us during the sandstorm. He had a loaded gun. We didn't. How could we argue?"

"I see," Conley said. "Well, now it's me that's got the loaded gun. If you're smart, you won't argue with me either."

"I wouldn't think of it, Marshal," Fannin said. "I know when to throw in a losing hand."

"You better. Head man at the pen said you were doing five years for rustling. That'll pass before you know it."

"Why, come to think of it, sure it will. Why didn't I think of that while I was in there?"

Conley caught his sarcasm and understood. Five years in the Yuma pen was five years in hell.

It must be especially hard for a woman, for Opal.

He said now to the Quechan, "How much time are you doing?"

"Ten year," Pascual said. "Eight more."

"Ten years for what?"

"I kill a Pima was mess around my woman."

"Only ten for murder?"

"Because I kill other Indian, see? It been white man, I get life."

Fannin looked at him. "You killed a man over a woman?"

Pascual met his look. "Best you remember that," he said.

"What the hell does that mean?"

Pascual simply shrugged.

In his own mind, Conley echoed Fannin's question. What did it mean? Would the Indian be protective of the girl in any kind of a showdown? Particularly against Fannin?

The thought brought an odd tinge of jealously to Ridge Conley.

And it brought back a remembrance of a time long ago. A time when he was a town marshal, twenty-one years old. A time when he was courting Kate Duncan there in the struggling little mining settlement of Taz.

He'd had serious intentions toward her.

And toward a career in law enforcement as well.

He had been proud even then of his job, though there was barely a need for it at that time in Taz. But he figured it as a step toward his future.

Kate, working as a seamstress, was not enthused. A job like his, she said, was a potential widow-maker.

"There are a lot of old lawmen around," Ridge had argued.

"And there are a lot more of them dead," Kate said.

And so his uneasy courtship had gone on for nearly a year.

Until the day Ross Brown, a wanted bank robber, rode in to rob the tiny Taz City Bank and got away with five hundred dollars in currency.

It was the biggest robbery in the town's short history.

And Ridge, with his eye open for opportunity, immediately gathered a small posse and led it off in the direction of Mexico, for which apparently Brown had fled.

The inexperienced posse rode back empty-handed the next day, with all its quick-fired enthusiasm gone.

Rode back to hear news worse than that of the bank being robbed.

Gabe Shaunessy, who ran the mercantile, was first to describe it to Conley.

"You hadn't been gone two hours when this stranger rode in," Shaunessy said. "Meanest-looking bastard you ever saw. His first stop was the saloon, right across the street from my store. According to those who were there, he ordered a bottle of rotgut and poured two-thirds of it down his throat like it was water." Gabe paused. "Big man, built like a bear."

"You in the saloon?" Ridge said.

"Not then," Gabe said. "Not till it was all over. That's when I needed a drink. Bad."

"When what was over?"

"Let me tell you what happened next," Shaunessy said. "I'd been looking out the front window of the store when the stranger rode in and tied up his horse at the saloon tie rack. Horse was a big, ugly roan, didn't look like it ever got much care."

Ridge said tightly, "Get on with what happened."

"I could hear things get quiet in the saloon soon as he went in. Well, it wasn't no more than five minutes before he came back out." Gabe shook his head. "Hard to believe a man could swallow a quart of Hugo's rotgut in that time, ain't it?"

Ridge waited.

"Like I said, he came right back out. Didn't appear to be staggering none, either, and went stomping down the walk there till he come to the front of Kate's dress shop."

"Kate's!" Ridge said. He grabbed Gabe's shirtfront.

"Dammit, Ridge! Let me go, you hear?"

"Kate all right?" Ridge let loose his grip.

Gabe scowled, then said, "He must have seen her through the shop window, it appeared. And went right in after her, like he had rape in mind."

"I should have been here to protect her!" Ridge said.

"I started down there on a run," Gabe said. "And then the explosion came. A Colt .45 blasting off."

Ridge couldn't speak.

"And that big stranger came walking back out the shop door, the whole front of him gushing blood, and fell dead in the street."

"And Kate?" Ridge said.

"Kate's fine. She's back in her shop right now. Might be best you get down there and hear it all from herself."

Later, he'd done that. But, somehow, what had happened had ruined what they'd had between them.

She'd needed protection, and he'd been gone off on a self-serving wild-goose chase when she needed him.

That was part of it. He understood that.

And in desperation she had killed a man with the Shop-keeper's Colt he had given her months before. "Just in case," he'd said with a smile, not believing she'd ever really have a need to use it.

That was the other part. A resentment that smoldered deep inside her that she had been forced to kill a man herself.

It erupted even as she gave him the account of the killing.

"If you had been here, I wouldn't live the rest of my life with the blood of that beast on my hands."

It was twisted thinking, he told himself. But it ended what

had been growing between them. She had withdrawn completely from him, and he had felt the loss deeply.

It had changed his attitude toward women. Never again had he recaptured the feeling he had once had for her.

He had satisfied his needs when and where he could, and remained a bachelor.

CHAPTER 8

AFTER serious thought, Conley agreed with Fannin's suggestion to take the northeasterly trace that led eventually to the border town of Sonoita.

He remained suspicious of Fannin's motives, but it did make sense, he decided. Whatever way they went, the toughest part would be missing sleep while trying to keep an eye on the prisoners.

It was long past sunrise when he finally got them started in that direction.

This time he left them unmanacled, Pascual going first, leading one pack animal. Fannin followed, leading the other.

Then the girl, walking now.

Conley brought up the rear, leading the buckskin. It was a hard way to go, but he could think of no better one. It was a strain on him, squinting ahead to forever keep an eye on the men.

He did not think they would make a break for it. After all, Fannin was going in the direction he wanted to go. And when, or if, a break came, he suspected it would be Fannin who would lead it.

The Quechan seemed resigned to his fate, but you never could tell about an Indian. Hell, Conley thought, you never could tell about a white man, either.

Or a woman.

So he kept alert during the beginning.

The hot, dusty miles fell behind, and his alertness faded.

He found his eyes more often resting on Opal. The days she had endured on the trail since the prison breakout had toughened her. He was surprised how well she kept up with the men.

And then he remembered something else about her. Before the trial she had told Conley that she'd been raised on a cattle ranch until her father had been forced out by an eastern combine. So the rough, outdoor life was not new to her. It was the prison confinement that she could not stand.

Like an Indian in that respect, he thought.

At that moment he shot a glance ahead to where the Quechan had been trudging, and discovered he was gone.

The pack burro continued along the trace, pushed onward by Fannin coming behind it.

Conley strode forward, moving fast past Opal, tugging the buckskin along. Past Fannin, too, who looked up with a grin as he went by.

"Lose something, Marshal?"

"Halt!"

"Sure, Marshal."

"When did he take off?"

"You don't really think I'd tell you that, do you?" Fannin said.

Conley looked around him.

Here was greasewood, thicker and heavier than it had been. There was some mesquite, too, as if its deep roots had tapped a modicum of water. Sometimes you found areas like this, spotted here and there over the more barren reaches of the desert.

The Indian had taken advantage of it to slip away.

"Never trust an Injun, Marshal," Fannin said.

"Never trust a convict, is more like it."

"That, too," Fannin said.

"Turn around."

Fannin turned the pack animal.

"Head back!"

Fannin did so, squeezing past Opal, who stood waiting.

Conley said, "Drop in behind him. Your Indian friend has disappeared." He paused. "Didn't you notice?"

"I noticed," she said.

"Makes it plain whose side you're on," he said.

"Of course. Did you really expect it to be different?"

"If I did, I was a fool."

"He helped me to escape. Do you think I'd turn against him?"

He gave it a brief thought, his eyes already searching the borders of the trace for sign of Pascual's exit.

"I guess not," he said. And despite his anger, he respected her for her conduct.

They had retraced their steps only a hundred yards when he spotted Pascual's tracks leading off to the east and disappearing in the brush.

Now he had a problem in what to do with Fannin and Opal while he took off to run down Pascual.

"You better hurry, Marshal," Fannin said. "That damn Injun could be moving fast."

That was true.

"When you live by the law, Marshal, you got all kinds of problems, ain't it so?"

Conley only half listened.

"That's why I gave up trying," Fannin said. "I figured being outside the law was simpler."

"Got you in the pen, didn't it?" Conley said.

"I hope you don't let that Injun get away. Him doing a murder sentence and all. He's the big-time one of us here. Wouldn't look right to your bosses was you to let him get away just to hold us short-timers." He looked at Opal. "Ain't that right, girl?"

She gave him a cold look.

"Killed a man over a woman, he did," Fannin said. "Now that ain't a right thing to do. That's a thing where you ought to see he pays for what he did."

"You don't shut up," Conley said, "I'm going to gag you."

"You want to get after that Injun, Marshal, tell you what to do. You tie me and the girl up together, real close like, so she can't get away."

"No!" Opal said.

"Why, girl, you don't know what you'd be missing."

That did it. Conley reached him in three steps, taking a set of manacles from his belt. He shoved his revolver into the convict's ribs.

"Turn around, hands in back!"

Fannin turned, and Conley snapped the cuffs on him.

"Lay down, facedown."

With Fannin in the prone, Conley pulled a tie rope from his pocket and lashed his ankles together.

Then he looked at the girl.

"What am I going to do with you?"

"Don't tie me close to *him*," she said.

Fannin laughed. "Like I said, you don't know what you'll be missing."

"I know."

Conley said to her, "Look, I'm going after Pascual. And there's always a chance I won't get back. I don't want to leave you out here helpless. So give me your word you won't run off."

"You'd do that for me?" she said.

"Give me your word."

"I do."

"Sounds like a wedding ceremony," Fannin said.

Conley ignored him. Moments later, mounted on the buckskin, he was tracking the Quechan.

He soon discovered that Pascual had headed for a vast expanse of jumbled lava, some of it in eroded thrusts still twenty feet in height. Interspersed among the basaltic formations were saguaros, ironwood, prickly pear cactus, and a natural pathway of sorts, into which Pascual's tracks disappeared.

Conley followed uneasily. On the lava pathway, there was

no sign of the Indian. Complicating this were other erosion-formed pathways, among which might be one taken by the fleeing man.

Why would he run off? Conley questioned. One reason would be to entice Conley to follow, so as to give Opal a chance to get free of capture. From what he had sensed of Pascual's feeling for the girl, the Indian might well have done this. Even if it left her in the hands of Fannin.

This was the sticker. Would Pascual do that?

Only if he intended to return to look after her, Conley thought. He swore at himself then. At that moment, he was almost certain the Quechan was trying to lead him into a trap to kill him.

Or maybe Pascual was only looking out for himself. Perhaps Conley had misjudged the man when it came to Opal, read something where there was nothing to read. In that case, Pascual could be once again striking south for deeper Mexico.

Abruptly he found himself out of the jumbled basalt, and just ahead was a lava-strewn bench with scrubby paloverde growing out of it.

And adjacent to the bench foot was a basaltic basin with water standing in it. Another *tinaja*.

Had Pascual known about this? He doubted it. Pascual might have already doubled back. Or fled on past.

As he debated this, he became aware that he was no longer alone. Behind him he sensed a presence. Pascual, he thought.

He turned slowly, thinking that Pascual could be armed with nothing more than a rock or a chunk of lava or a piece of ironwood. He could be dangerous, though, even thus.

He was stunned by what he saw.

A Mexican in the garb of a Rurale crouched half hidden in a fissure of the twisted lava. Only his hat and his jacket showed. His hat and his jacket and his revolver. He wore a sergeant's insignia.

"Drop your *pistola, ladròn!*" he said.

Ladròn, Conley thought. Means thief. He hesitated.

"*Now, hombre!* I have two other men ready to shoot."

From somewhere off to Conley's right, one of them called, "You believe it, gringo!"

Conley lifted his gun with his fingertips and let it fall.

"So," the Rurale sergeant said. He stepped out from his cover. "Our long chase is over, you gringo *bastardo,*" he said.

"Chase for who?" Conley said.

"You, *ladròn.*"

"I'm not a thief, *amigo.*"

"No? What you call yourself, then? A borrower?"

"I don't understand, friend."

"You pretty stupid, then. We have chase you all the way from Hermosillo. After you steal that horse you riding from Don Luis Quijada. And try to rob his bank." He paused. "We been Rural Police."

"So I see," Conley said. "And in my pocket I carry the star of a United States deputy marshal."

"So you steal badges, too, eh?"

"And my identification."

"You been busy steal things, I see," the Rurale said.

"I speak the truth."

"So? So do I, *gabacho.* We are going to show you what we do when we catch a gringo *ladròn* who steals the favorite horse of Don Luis."

"I did not steal him," Conley said. "It was stolen by a bandit named Kuster."

"You make joke? Custer he been killed ten, twelve year. Indians kill him at Little Big Horn. Even in Méjico we hear about that."

"Not that Custer."

"*That* I believe," Razo said. "He been dead twelve year."

"Let me show you my marshal's star. And my identification card."

"Go ahead. Show. No tricks, you die."

Conley reached carefully into a pocket and drew forth his badge. He held it up for the Rurale to see.

"It maybe been stole," Razo said.

Conley reached again and got a thin, leather card case.

"*Identificación*," he said, holding it out.

"Maybe stole too."

"You don't *want* to believe me," Conley said bitterly.

"You been right, *ladrón*. It make our work more easy, we just take you back with us. You and the fine horse."

"What kind of lawmen are you?" Conley said.

"I told you. We been Rurales."

The others had come out of hiding, and stood beside Razo.

The one called Chuy said, "We have ridden hard, and have suffered thirst and hunger. It would please me, *sargento*, to shoot off his *huevos* right now."

"No," the sergeant said. "We will bring him to Don Luis. Don Luis will be appreciative of that. I am certain Don Luis will invite us to attend a private execution."

Pascual had almost blundered into the Mexican riders himself. Then, staying out of sight, he witnessed their confrontation with the marshal.

He could not hear all the conversation between them, but seeing their leader pointing at the buckskin horse, he guessed at what was happening. Those Rurales had mistaken the marshal for that one on the run who called himself Kuster. The one the marshal had killed.

Things were working out better than he, Pascual, had dared to hope. His flight from the Sonoita trail had been an impulsive thing, not really thought through. He had hoped to lead Conley astray, perhaps lose him temporarily in the *malpais*. Maybe even capture the horse. At least to cause him to spend time searching fruitlessly while he himself swung back to rejoin Opal.

Hopefully then they would have regained a lead on the lawman, with a chance to again escape.

Now these Rurales had solved everything for him.

He slipped away, heading back to rejoin the others.

He was surprised when he reached them to find Fannin trussed, but Opal waiting free.

She was startled at his reappearance.

"You came back!" she said.

He nodded. "I come back for you," he said.

She seemed not to hear. "What have you done with the marshal?"

"I do nothing."

"Did you see him?"

He sensed the concern in her voice.

"Don't worry," he said. "He don't come back."

"What do you mean?"

He studied her closely. "You worry about that?"

She did not answer at once. Then she said, *"Why won't he come back?"*

He kept looking at her in silence. Then he nodded. "So!" he said. He paused, then said, "Messican police take him. Rurales. Think he one steal horse."

"But he's a lawman too!"

Pascual shrugged. "They don't believe, maybe. Don't care, maybe."

"Rurales," she said. "They'll shoot him on the spot!"

"I hear some what they say. They take him back to Hermosillo."

Fannin had got himself to a sitting position. "Dammit!" he said. "Get me loose, you hear?"

"Maybe I leave you like that," Pascual said.

"Leave me? What the hell kind of a white man are you?"

"Not white," Pascual said. "Me Injun, remember?"

"All right, dammit!" Fannin said. "I was forgetting."

Pascual looked at him. "First time you forget, hey?"

"Come on, man. Untie me."

"You can't leave him like that to die," Opal said.

"You got good heart," Pascual said. He frowned then. "Too bad for you."

But he bent over Fannin and untied his ankles.

Fannin stood up, weaving as he got his balance. "Now the cuffs. How we going to get them off?"

"The marshal left a key with me," Opal said. "In case he never got back, I was to let you loose."

"Damn your eyes," Fannin said. "You held out on me, girl."

"He was afraid I'd not survive alone," she said.

"What the hell is going on between you and that badge toter?"

She handed the key to Pascual, but she didn't answer the question. She couldn't. She didn't know, herself.

She knew one thing, though. She was worried about Ridge Conley being in the hands of those Rurales.

They resumed their plodding way along the trace. Pascual did not argue for his earlier choice of heading south into Sonora. His close encounter with the Rurales had apparently changed his mind.

Now, if anything, he seemed in a hurry to put distance between himself and where he had left the Mexicans.

Fannin thought about this, and after a time, when they stopped for drink and a short rest, he spoke of it.

"The pace you're setting, Injun, them Rurales must have put a scare into you."

Pascual said nothing.

"What I hear, they're hell on Injuns," Fannin said, "even though some of them are mostly Injun, their own self. Just as rough on their own kind as on anybody else. Maybe even rougher. Shows what can happen when you pin a badge of authority on a man."

It gave Opal something to think about. She wondered what Ridge Conley would be like without his lawman's star.

After all these years, would he be the same even without

the badge? Was his code of conduct so deeply ingrained by now that nothing could ever change it?

Would she always be to him an ex-convict, even if she served her time?

She was brought up short by the thought. Whatever was she even vaguely contemplating? Some sort of relationship in the future?

She felt herself flushing. The desert heat must be driving her mad, she thought.

Even the idea was insane. Wasn't he on his way now to a summary justice at the hands of the dreaded Rurales? The stories she'd heard about Dìaz's police did not bode well for his survival.

She was made despondent by the thought.

Fannin's voice came to her then. "On your feet, girl. We got miles to cover."

Conley was trying to make the Rurale believe him. "I tell you, Sergeant, I took the horse from the *ladròn*."

"What you do with him, then?"

"I killed him in a gunfight."

"When?"

"A day ago. Listen, I can take you to his body. It is at the *tinaja* of the Papagos. You could take the body back to the Don."

Razo tapped his finger against his aquiline nose. "In such heat? *Hombre*, I got a strong stomach, but not that strong."

The Rurale Chuy had been listening, and now he spoke.

"Don't listen to this gringo, *jefe*."

"Listen, you," Razo said, "don't tell me what to do."

"I only suggest," Chuy said.

"Don't suggest."

"*Sì, jefe*."

Razo said then, to Conley, "You have no business here in Méjico. Even if you are a *mariscal* of the Estados Unidos, what do you do in our country?"

"I came after prisoners who escaped from the prison at Yuma."

"The prison at Yuma," Razo said. "I hear about it. I hear a prisoner can't escape from there."

"Not true. I came after"—he hesitated—"two who did."

"And where they are now?"

"Not far. Maybe four, five miles."

Razo seemed to give this some thought.

He said, "There is reward for them?"

"Yes. Fifty dollars apiece, American."

"Not enough."

He had to stall them, Conley thought. And he had to get back to the convicts before they got away.

In desperation then, he said, "And they have abducted a fine-looking woman from the town of Yuma."

"She is with them yet?" Razo said.

"Yes."

Chuy spoke up again. "It has been a long time, *jefe*, since we had a woman."

"It might be worth a ride of a few extra miles," Razo said. "Mount up!" he said to his men.

Then, to Conley, he said, "Lead us to them, gringo. We will see if you are telling the truth."

Conley gestured to his revolver, still lying where he'd dropped it. "They are desperate men," he said. "I will need a gun."

"We got guns," Razo said.

"Even so."

Razo said to Chuy, "Get him his gun. But take out the bullets first. And keep his cartridge belt."

"An empty gun is not much use," Conley said. He stuffed the weapon in his waistband.

"You can bluff them with it," Razo said. "But there won't be a need."

Conley was already thinking he'd made a mistake in telling them about the woman.

He had used her as bait to excite their lusts, and now he regretted it.

Mounted, they came up close behind the convicts within the hour.

Razo said, "Gringo, you say they don't got guns?"

"That's right."

"And how I know you don't lie some more?"

Conley shrugged. "You don't. But if I close in, and they are armed, they'll shoot at me, no?"

"If you are the marshal, yes."

"So?"

"Go ahead, gringo."

Conley rode in, looking bold but not feeling so.

What if somehow one of them had found cartridges for Kuster's gun? he thought. He'd emptied it, stuck it in one of the packs, and pocketed the few cartridges remaining in Kuster's belt back there at the Papago Tanks. But now the scant possibility disturbed him, unlikely as it was.

They heard him coming and turned and saw the Rurales waiting a short distance behind.

Fannin and Pascual showed dismay. Opal's expression was a mixture of dismay and relief that Conley was unharmed.

Had he made some sort of deal with the Rurales? she wondered.

"Talk about a bad penny showing up," Fannin said bitterly. "And with greaser police to boot." He paused. "You must make friends fast."

The Rurales rode in then, while the convicts watched them come.

Sergeant Razo was in the lead, and as he halted a few paces away his eyes swept the men and came to rest on Opal.

He said, "Well, gringo, you told the truth about the woman, all right. *Muy bonita.* Very pretty."

CHAPTER 9

CONLEY said, "You see they all wear the clothes of convicts."

He was trying to divert Razo's attention from the girl.

Chuy said, "Even in such clothes, she looks good to me, *jefe*."

Opal's expression hardened. She said to Conley, "Why did you lead them here?"

Razo grinned. It was plain he understood English well enough. He said, "Feel flattered, *muchacha*. He tell us how pretty you been, and so we come to see you."

She still faced Conley. "Why?" she said again.

He said, "I'm sorry. They were taking me to Hermosillo. It was the only way I could think to stop them."

"So you bought your life by selling mine," she said.

"I shouldn't have done it," he said. "I regret it now."

Razo, who had been listening closely, smiled. He said, "Don't be hard on him, *muchacha*. We was take him back to shoot for horse thief."

Anger remained on her face.

"I tell you someting, *muchacha*," Razo said then. "Don't be fret. Maybe you have revenge for what he done. Maybe we take him back anyway, to be shot." He paused. "After we make pleasure with you first."

Conley said, "As a lawman, how can you condone rape?"

"We show you," Razo said. "We let you watch."

He turned to Chuy. "But first tie up these others."

Chuy said, "What about the *mariscal*?"

Razo looked thoughtful, then he grinned. "Leave him free while he watches. With an empty gun, what can he do, even if he had the courage? Let the girl know what kind of *hombre* he is. It will make the enjoyment better."

"*Jefe*," Chuy said, "you give me the surprise sometimes."

"I get my pleasures maybe in different ways," Razo said.

Fannin was quickly tied.

But the big Quechan struggled until it took all of them to wrestle him to the ground and hold him down.

Conley was forgotten and ignored. His hand slid into his pocket and withdrew the bullets he'd taken from Kuster's gun back at the Papago tanks. He slipped his empty six-gun from his waistband, swung the cylinder open.

One of the Rurales, his weight on the Indian, started to glance his way, but just then Pascual gave a final desperate shrug that nearly upset those pinning him.

Unseen, Conley got the chambers filled as Chuy slammed his pistol barrel against the Quechan's temple. They had Pascual tied before he recovered from the jolt.

He had guts, Pascual did, Conley thought. Let's see what I've got.

Razo had already grabbed Opal and thrown her to the ground. He had unfastened his pants and was pinning her beneath him as she struggled. Chuy was watching intently.

The other Rurale glanced at Conley, saw his gun in hand, and grabbed for his own. Conley fired and dropped him.

Chuy turned at the sound, drew, fired in haste, and missed. Conley put him down with a bullet in his heart.

He swung back then to the sergeant.

Razo, his pants down over his legs, was scrambling for his discarded belt and gun.

Opal kicked at his hip, knocking him flat.

Conley stepped close to avoid wounding her, and from four feet away shot Razo in the head.

Fannin, from where he lay bound, saw this and said, "Christ!"

Now they had horses, and all could ride.

There was some food, too, in the Rurales' saddlebags. Dried-out tortillas, but edible, a kind of beef jerky flavored with chili, a few small sacks of dried beans. And each horse carried across its pommel a grain bag with a couple of days' forage of corn remaining, of which Conley immediately gave a ration to the hard-used buckskin.

And canteens of water, filled at the lava waterhole.

But before Conley could take once again to the trail with his prisoners, he had a job to do. He had to get rid of the bodies.

They had no way to bury them, no way to dig without tools. They had to hide the evidence of the killings if they were to make it safely back across the border.

Conley scouted around briefly for some other means. A hundred yards east of the trace he found a sharp, narrow arroyo.

He went back to the others and said to the men, "All right, we'll drag them over there." He gestured in that direction.

It was a job none relished.

They threw the corpses into the dry wash, then broke away the edge of a cutbank, kicking it loose with their boots, to cover them. It was the best they could do.

Once done, Conley got them mounted, tied again, and ready to move. He swung onto Razo's horse, leading the buckskin to give it rest.

"I want you to know," Fannin said, "that I only helped hide them dead Rurales to save my own neck. We're still in Mexico, where we hadn't ought to be. Any more of their kind come roaming around and stumble onto what's happened here, and it'll be a fast end for all of us."

"So we better get moving," Conley said. "You keep in mind what you just said. The sooner we get back across the border now, the safer we'll be."

"Let's don't waste time talking," Opal said. She was visibly distraught by what had happened.

Pascual, listening to them converse, seemed to have lost all inclination to go south. It was as if he had decided that American law was preferable to that of Mexico.

"Lead off," Conley told him. "But don't try any more damn tricks."

"You shoot fast," the Quechan said. He appeared to be thinking about the men that Conley had just killed.

"Don't forget that," Conley said.

Fannin appeared to be thinking about it too, but he said nothing as they started up the trace again.

Once he looked back at Conley, and in the distance behind him he saw a pall of dust arising, as if another sandstorm was raging down there. Down where Conley had shot Kuster, maybe.

Yes, he thought, the marshal was damn quick with a gun. Too quick, maybe.

At the Mexican town of Caborca, some eighty miles southeast of the Papago tanks, there was a small garrison of soldiers. The garrison consisted of a lieutenant, a sergeant, a corporal who was the lieutenant's orderly, and four privates.

One of the privates was the Sand Papago they called Juanito Carbajal, who had been personally recruited by the garrison commander, Lieutenant Montoya.

Private Carbajal, often called simply Juanito, held a limbo position in the cadre, looked down upon slightly because of his roots, yet accepted readily enough because he had knowledge of that hostile land to the west that they had, on occasion, to venture reluctantly.

All they really knew about him, or cared to know, was that he had been brought down from Arizona to the Pinacate by his parents, and had lived there for several years, becoming familiar with the terrain.

They knew that, growing into manhood, he had explored the region as had few others since his ancestors had departed it.

And that after his parents, too, had deserted their tiresome attempt to exist at Papago tanks, Juanito had shunned a return to reservation life, and had come to Caborca, seeking work.

It was here then that Lieutenant Montoya, learning of his background, recruited him as a replacement for one of his soldiers killed in a cantina brawl.

He could use such a man as Juanito for a guide when, where, or if needed. The need, once in a while, arose as outlaws preying on Sonoran towns fled into the desert for temporary refuge.

The garrison at Caborca was where the Rurales had stopped a couple of days previously to replenish their supplies and to trade for fresh horses.

The lieutenant had accommodated them because they brought with them orders, signed by his own colonel in Hermosillo, that he was to do so.

He had little liking for their kind. They were often no more than marauders themselves, he thought, incorporated into the federal police force by Dìaz to enforce a ruthless dictatorship.

But the lieutenant was smart enough to obey orders.

Thus, when he later received a courier's message from Magdalena, where there was a telegraph, he read it with a frown.

His orderly, having handed him the message, watched this, and said, "Bad news, *mi teniente?*"

"A pain in the *culo*," the lieutenant said. "Another order from the colonel that we are to give all possible assistance to those damned *verdugos* who passed through here."

The corporal knew the lieutenant, who had graduated from the army academy at Chapultepec, had no use for the methods of the Rurales. That was why he called them *verdugos*, slang for executioners.

"So they are gone, *teniente*. So we are free from having to help, isn't it true, sir?"

The lieutenant was thoughtful. "In a way, yes. Still, when the colonel sends such an order, it isn't wise to do nothing." He paused. "It appears the *verdugos* were send on their mission at the request of Don Luis Quijada."

"Don Luis, sir?"

"I forgot, you are from Chihuahua," the lieutenant said. "Don Luis Quijada is *muy importante* down Hermosillo way. Big *hacendado,* and all that. And, it seems, a personal friend of our colonel." He paused. "So we had better make at least a gesture of complying with that request."

"What can you do now, sir? The Rurales are somewhere in the desert, on the trail of that *ladròn* they said they were seeking."

The lieutenant gave that more thought. "I will send the Papago to find them. With a couple of men. And orders to help them in their search. That should satisfy the colonel's instructions."

"Can you trust the Papago, sir?"

"I'll send Sergeant Herrera in command."

"Shall I send them in, sir?"

"Do it at once."

The Papago, who sometimes grew bored with the routine of garrison life, had two days before watched the departure of the three Rurales.

In fact, he had given them information as to the possible route taken by their quarry. They had previously, by inquiry at stops along the way up from Hermosillo, traced him thus far to Caborca.

From here the obvious trail went northwesterly to Sonoita. However, a man trying to lose pursuers, a man on a tiring horse, guessing they might acquire fresh mounts at the garrison and overtake him, could try to lose himself in the desert to the west.

So, as he led the way of Sergeant Hererra and another

soldier named Salas, Juanito kept close scrutiny along the side of the trail. He was a short, stocky young man.

Eventually, after some twenty miles, he halted his companions. He pointed to hoofprints in the sand leading westward. There was even a faint trail of sorts going that direction.

"There," he said.

"You know where they're heading?" the sergeant said.

"I think so, *sargento*. The man they hunt, he maybe knows something of the desert. That trail is a way to the *tinajas* once belonged to my people."

"Follow it," Hererra said.

In the afternoon the sun disappeared early, and Juanito gestured ahead to where the horizon was obscured by dust.

"There been another sandstorm, I think," he said. "Maybe now, maybe yesterday. And maybe those Rurales get lost."

"Serve them right," Herrera said.

"You don't like Rurales, *sargento*?"

"Who does?" the sergeant said.

They made a dry camp that night, and in the morning the sky had partly cleared. In late afternoon, they reached the *tinajas*.

At their approach, a wild flight of buzzards took to the air.

"Ay, *cabrones!*" Salas said.

They could see there was much flesh missing from the body of Kuster. Both his eyes had been pecked out.

Hererra covered his nostrils with a handkerchief, and went over to study the corpse.

He came back and said, "Hard to say."

"Hard to say what, *sargento*?"

"Hard to say if this is the one the Rurales were after. They had a description of the *ladròn* that I heard them giving to the lieutenant. This one could fit it, I think, before he was half eaten."

"*Maldito* buzzards!" Salas said.

"You speak of the birds or the Rurales?" Hererra said.

"Is there a difference?" Salas said.

They watered the mounts and themselves, then Juanito studied their surroundings. The sandstorm had obliterated most tracks. But he found some prints in a protected spot where the trail began toward the northeast.

"Whoever was here," he said, "they went that way."

"Follow them," Hererra said.

As they rode up the trail, the drifted sand lessened. It appeared that the most recent storm had not ranged as widely as the earlier ones. Soon Juanito was reading trail sign left by a horse, two pack animals, three men, and what appeared to have been a woman.

He was puzzled, and said so to the sergeant. "Lot of people. What they doing out here?"

"You're the tracker," Hererra said. "You tell me."

The Papago shook his head. "Can't tell," he said.

He rode with his eyes on the trail, wondering. The miles went by.

Suddenly he halted.

"Now what?" Hererra said. He was getting tired of the whole thing. He didn't like the desert. He liked garrison life, and the cantinas at Caborca.

Juanito didn't answer at once. Instead, he spent a quarter hour scrutinizing the medley of prints.

"Well?" the sergeant said. He was sounding impatient.

"I see like this," Juanito said. "One man, he leave party on foot. Rest go on. Then rest come back. One man he leave on horse to follow first man who left." He paused.

"Go on."

"First man, he come back. Then man who rode after, he ride back. Only now there three other riders with him."

"You can tell all that from those tracks?" Hererra said.

"I tell more," Juanito said. "Those other riders, their horse prints been same as the Rurales'."

Hererra had dismounted, and now he was studying the confusion of prints himself.

He said, "Those dark splotches scattered around, that's blood!"

The Papago nodded. "Plenty blood, Sergeant. Look over there."

Juanito crossed to where he'd pointed. He bent down and picked up what appeared to be a broken bit of pottery. He held it up. "It been piece of skull," he said.

"Ay, *Cristo!*" Salas said.

Hererra kept staring at what Carbajal held in his hand.

Finally, he pulled his eyes away. "What about this other blood?" he said.

"One Rurale die there," Juanito said, pointing. "Another die over there."

"I think the Rurales all dead," the sergeant said. "Who did it?"

Juanito stepped over to stand covering another set of prints. "I think it was man standing here," he said.

"He must be one *gran pistolero*," Salas said.

"So where are the bodies?" Hererra said.

"I find," the Papago said. He could see where they had been dragged off the trail.

"This way," he said.

The others followed. He led them to the arroyo, saw the broken cutbank, and slipped down into the wash.

With his bare hands he began digging into the sand.

Within moments he had bared a Rurale's face, turned upward the way the corpse had fallen.

Instantly, he shrank away from it. He was a Papago, and Papagos had a fear of handling the dead.

He came clambering out of the wash.

"Hold on!" Hererra said. "I want to see the others."

"Let Salas dig," Juanito said. "I don't like dead people. They got ghosts can come bothering if you touch."

The sergeant said, "I thought it was Navajos that had that belief."

"Us Papagos," Juanito said. "We got it too."

"Salas?" Hererra said.

"Me, *sargento?*"

"You!"

"I never told you before," Salas said. "But I got some Papago blood myself. It's on my grandmother's side, Sergeant."

"Get your *culo* down there and dig," Hererra said. "You got any Indian blood, it's Yaqui."

Conley was not pushing the pace. He wanted to conserve the strength of the animals for the long trip back. He stopped frequently for rests.

Each time, he studied Opal to see how she was making it. And each time he was surprised at her apparent stamina.

She was strong, he thought, a strong and resilient woman. She would have made some man a good wife if she hadn't made that single, foolish mistake that time of the stagecoach.

Or even *with* that mistake . . . If he hadn't brought her in.

He remembered old Hap Hanson, the driver, pleading that he let her go.

But he'd had his professional code. . . .

Suddenly, he called to the convicts, "All right, let's go!"

All of them turned, startled at the bitter anger in his voice.

The two men only glanced, then struggled to get up on their saddles, grasping the horns with manacled hands to help.

Opal, unmoving, held his stare with curious eyes. Then, slowly, her curiosity faded, replaced with a shocked surprise.

After a long moment she turned from him and went to the horse he had given her.

She mounted quickly. He had left her hands free.

There was a faint frown on her face, as if she wasn't sure whether to be pleased or disturbed by what she had seen.

"At the trot, *hombres!*" Sergeant Hererra ordered. "I want to catch up to those *cabrones* who murdered the officers of the law."

Salas said, "You mean the *verdugos?*"

"Who else?" Hererra said. "Our lieutenant had orders from his colonel that we are to provide help."

"But they are dead," Salas said.

"Then we have to arrest their killers."

"At least one of them is an excellent *pistolero,*" Salas said.

"I do not intend to go back empty-handed with the story of what we found at the arroyo," the sergeant said. "I can imagine what the lieutenant would say. Worse yet, how the colonel would take it. I like the cantinas at Caborca. There are many worse places to be posted. Places with no cantinas. Places with no whores to take care of a man's needs."

"I think I understand, *sargento,*" Salas said.

"Good. When we catch up, I expect you and Carbajal to act like soldiers."

"You would have us shoot them?"

"Only," Hererra said, "if they resist."

"I have never shot a man," the Papago soldier said.

"There is a first time for any soldier, if he stays in the army long enough," the sergeant said.

"You have killed, then?"

"I have killed."

"How many men, sergeant?"

"Who knows? I killed in battle action. In the confusion of battle, you don't have time to keep count. You shoot at the enemy, and more often than not you do not know when you hit and when you miss, because there are others shooting beside you."

"I would think," Juanito said, "that would be a good thing. Not to know, I mean."

For a long moment, Hererra was silent. Then he said, "Yes, *muchacho.* It is a good thing, if you don't know. In after years· you may sleep better." He paused. "And maybe you won't drink so much."

CHAPTER 10

CONLEY, bringing up the rear, glanced behind him frequently. He was driven by a haunting concern over what he had been forced to do back there. To kill a Rurale, in Dìaz's Mexico, was to write your own death warrant, he knew.

A warrant that would be effective if ever his guilt became known. And he was not at all certain his act could long be hidden.

And even if it was, he had another worry. The convicts, their escape thwarted by his capture of them, were eyewitness to what he had done. He had no hope that they would remain silent if it was to their advantage to reveal what happened.

Suppose he succeeded in taking them back to Yuma? Facing those high walls and barred gate for years to come, would any of them remain silent?

Even if he had left Mexico behind, they could raise a storm for the sake of vengeance. A storm that could grow, quite possibly, into an international incident. He tried to recall if there was an extradition agreement between the two countries.

Fannin, especially, would delight in making trouble for him.

Pascual would undoubtedly do so in retribution for the heavy sentence he would have to serve.

And the girl, with her terror of confinement—he could not believe she would act differently, despite the fact it was his protecting her that caused his predicament.

It was *possible*, though, that she would remain silent, he thought. How could you tell what a woman would do? After what happened in that time long ago between Kate Duncan and himself . . . He could never forget that.

But even if she did not talk, what would it matter? The talk of the other two would be enough. It could mean the end of his career. For the first time he could see how bringing them back to prison could destroy him as a law-enforcement officer.

That was irony for you! he thought.

It kind of played hell with his profesional code.

The hell with all that! he thought then. He would live by his code, no matter what. He would put them back behind those walls, because that's where the law had decreed they should be.

One way to go, and only one, that was how he had to live his life.

No matter what the risk. No matter what the consequences.

As always, once he decided thusly based on his personal credo, it freed his mind for the job at hand. Which was to bring his prisoners back.

But it did not free him from the concern that kept him looking back over his shoulder.

Opal kept thinking about Conley as she rode.

Thinking about what she'd seen in his eyes, and how she might use it. Use it to her advantage.

When they next stopped to rest, she avoided his glance, afraid he might read her thoughts. She did not want him to be suspicious of her. If she was to use him, she'd have to do it with finesse. A finesse she doubted she possessed.

Presently, he walked into the brush to relieve himself, and Fannin spoke.

"Listen, girl," he said. "You're our chance of getting free."

"What do you mean?"

"I can't tell you now. Marshal will be coming back in a minute. But you can see he favors you considerable. No manacles. And he trusted you to stay put after he tied me up. Someplace along the trail, there'll be a chance to use this."

She was startled by his words, expressing almost what she herself had been thinking.

Pascual was listening, his face, as usual, inexpressive.

Conley was walking back, and Fannin fell into silence.

But first he said, in a low, quick voice, "I'm thinking of a time after we've passed through Sonoita."

Conley stood there, looking at them, studying them as if he had heard their conversation, although she knew he hadn't.

It made her nervous.

"Something bothering you, Opal?" he said.

"I've got plenty to be bothered about, haven't I?"

He had no answer for that, and he said, "Let's move on."

The sound of horsemen at that moment turned him rigid.

He whirled about, gun drawn, as the three Mexican soldiers appeared a short distance away.

"*Hola!*" the one in the lead shouted. "We want to talk!"

Conley recognized their uniforms. He wanted no trouble with the Mexican army. Especially now. He slid his weapon back in its holster.

The soldiers rode up.

The sergeant said, "*Norteamericanos,* eh?" He looked at the handcuffed men and at their convict clothes. Then he looked at Opal. He addressed Conley again. "Your captives, eh? You are a *cazador por enganche,* a bounty hunter?"

Conley reached slowly to withdraw his marshal's star from his pocket. He showed it. "Mariscal de los Estados Unidos," he said.

"Ahhh!" The sergeant did not smile. "And what do you do in our country?"

The same old question, Conley thought. Forty years since the Mexican-American War, and they have not yet forgotten.

He said, "These are escapees from the prison at Yuma. I was sent to bring them back."

"Have you seen three mounted Rurales in the vicinity?"

"Rurales?" Conley said.

"Yes," Fannin said. "He saw them all right." His border Spanish wasn't the best, but the sergeant seemed to understand him.

The sergeant said, "Tell me about it, *hombre.*"

"He killed them," Fannin said.

As if by signal, all three soldiers had weapons out and pointed at Conley.

"Is it true?" the sergeant said to him.

Conley said, "There was a reason."

"What reason for murder?"

"Not murder. They drew on me. It was them or me."

"They were *federal* police. They had that right."

"Their *jefe* was raping the woman there," Conley said, nodding toward her.

"Not unknown among Rurales," the sergeant said.

He turned his attention toward Opal. "Is this true, woman?"

She did not understand Spanish. She turned to Conley.

"What did he say?"

"Wants to know if what I said is true."

"Well, what *did* you say?"

"I told him I killed the Rurales because they were raping you," he said.

Fannin spoke up harshly."This is our chance, girl, a chance they'll arrest him and let us go. Tell him the marshal lies."

"How?" she said.

"Shake you head, and say, *es mentira.* Means it is a lie."

The sergeant had been looking from one to another.

Now he said, "I understand a small English, woman. Is true what the Rurales done at you?"

"It is true," she said. "The marshal saved me."

Fannin said to her, "You stupid fool! I thought you had some sense."

The soldier, Salas, said, "What is going on, *sargento?*"

Hererra, still keeping his eyes on Conley, told him.

"What are you going to do?"

"We'll have to take him back to Caborca."

Conley, listening, said, "I told you they were all set on raping the woman. The *jefe* had already begun."

"You will be given a hearing. There will be an inquiry. Maybe a trial." The sergeant paused. "You understand this is the best I can do for you? I was sent to find the Rurales. And to help them catch a man who committed a crime in Hermosillo."

"That man is dead. At the tank of the Papagos."

"So that is the one. We saw him. The Rurales killed him?"

Fannin spoke up again. "No, the marshal killed him too!"

The soldiers still had Conley covered with their revolvers.

"We will take that *pistola* of yours," Hererra said. "Get it, Salas. There appears to be a lot of tiger in this man."

Salas went close and said, "With the fingertips, hombre."

He took the weapon. "What about the others, *sargento*? We take them to Caborca too?"

"Yes. They were witnesses to what happened."

"We will take the pack animals, of course?"

"Of course."

"It will be a bother."

"It will make us look good when we reach the garrison," Hererra said.

Juanito said, "Shall we backtrack, *sargento*? Back the way we came?"

"Is there a shorter way?"

"Yes, there are old Papago trails all over the Pinacate, if you know where to look."

"You know?"

"I can find us a good route that will take us to the Caborca road."

"Find it."

"We will backtrack a short way, then we will come to it."

"Get on with it, I said."

"*Sì, sargento,*" the Papago said. Presently, he had them on the way.

But this time, Conley wore the third set of manacles.

From time to time as he led the way, Juanito cast his glance behind him to where Pascual followed, leading the convict party in progression. The sergeant and Salas brought up the rear, so as to keep a watch on the extended group.

Each time the Papago looked back, he met the eyes of Pascual and briefly held his stare.

A time came when he dropped back to ride beside him.

He said in Spanish, "You are Quechan?"

Pascual nodded.

"I am Papago. Sand Papago. Once my people were of the branch called by the Spanish Pinacateños."

"I have heard," Pascual said. "Quechan people have been friends with the Pinacatenos in the old days."

"So my father once told me," Juanito said. "Is it true that the *mariscal* killed those Rurales?"

"Yes, it is true. But he did it because of the woman."

"He has been taking you back to the prison?"

"That, too, is true."

"Then you must hate him."

"For that, yes. Still he does a job. And he saved the woman from the Rurales."

"Ah," Juanito said, "the Rurales. A necessary evil in a land as vast as Mexico, I suppose. Did you know that Dìaz patterned them, originally, after the Texas Rangers, who he admired?"

"Has the pattern changed?"

Juanito was silent before he answered. "There are both good and bad among those who administer the law. Being a convict, you should know that. What I have seen, though, is that the bad ones can be very bad."

Pascual was silent.

The Papago went on. "Would you say the Rurales that the *mariscal* killed, would you say they were bad ones?"

"Why do you ask?"

"I am thinking of you. You and your *amigos*," Juanito said. "It will go very hard for the marshal if he killed *good* Rurales. You understand? He could be executed for murder. In that case, you might well be freed."

"So?"

"You are a witness. It is for you to say whether or not he was right in killing them."

"He was," Pascual said. "It was the only way he could save the woman."

Juanito frowned. "You had better give it some more thought, amigo. You are Indian like me. Indians don't live long in prison. I am telling you a way so you won't die there."

Pascual did not speak at once. Then he said, *"Gracias, amigo.* I will give it thought, as you say."

"You had better do it," the Papago said.

Caborca was a typical Sonoran town of adobes.

They reined up in front of the garrison headquarters.

Lieutenant Montoya, alerted of their approach by his orderly, stood out front waiting. He was a young and virile man, and his eyes quickly picked out the woman among them.

"What have we there?" he said to the corporal.

The orderly knew he wasn't supposed to answer, and remained silent.

Sergeant Hererra dismounted and saluted.

"Who are these gringo convicts?" Montoya said.

"It is a long story, *teniente,*" Hererra said.

The guardhouse was no better or worse than you might expect of a Mexican jail, Conley thought. He was judging by what he had heard over the years. This was his first experience of being in one.

He was alone in his cell. Adjoining his was one containing Fannin and Pascual. Beyond them, Opal was in the last of a row of three. All faced a long bare adobe wall, which formed the side of a corridor fronting the cells. There were adobe walls between the cells too, so that he could not see any of the others.

He could not see them, but he could hear them.

Almost at once, it was Fannin's voice that sought him out.

"Little taste of what it's like, Marshal," Fannin said. "How do you like it?"

Conley didn't answer.

"How'd you like to spend years of *your* life in one of these cages? You think about that. Then you think about all the men you've brought in to do just that. If you got any conscience at all, that ought to weigh on it." He paused. "Hell, you may get life for shooting those Rurales. That's if they don't shoot you." Another pause. "You hearing me, Conley?"

Conley heard him. But his mind wasn't on Fannin's question. It was on what he'd said about bringing people in.

Specifically, bringing Opal in.

"Conley?" Fannin sounded irked that he'd got no answer.

"I heard you, goddammit!" Conley said.

He heard Fannin laugh.

There was a short silence before Fannin spoke again.

"Maybe we can deal, Marshal," he said.

"What do you mean, *deal?*"

"A trade-off. These Mexes are going to hang your balls unless you got a damn good reason for shooting those Rurales."

"I've got a good reason. You saw it all yourself."

"That I did, Marshal, that I did," Fannin said. "The thing is there's a couple different ways I might have seen it."

"Like what?"

"Like the way it really happened. The way you'll tell it.

And then there's the way I might tell it. With the Injun, here, to back me up. And the girl, too."

"Why would they lie?"

"Come on, Marshal. You ain't that stupid. Once they shoot you, they'll turn us free."

"And if you tell the truth?"

"If we back your story, we want your promise to leave us be. Go back empty-handed, and tell that frigging warden you lost our trail in the sandstorm."

"The girl already told the truth to the sergeant," Conley said. "She will back me up."

"Believe that if you want, Marshal."

"I believe it."

"Then you're a fool. When she said that, it was before she had this taste of being locked up again. I been listening to her pacing that cell on the other side of me. A caged tigress is what she is, Marshal. The girl suffers from claustrophobia, did you know that? That means she'll say *anything* to stay out of a prison cell."

Conley was silent again. He knew there could be truth in what Fannin said.

"You think it over, Marshal," Fannin said. "You think it over real good."

"Let me talk to Pascual."

"No need, Marshal. He agrees with what I said."

"Let me hear him."

Pascual spoke up. "Better you listen what he say. You promise let us go. We tell truth."

Fannin spoke again. "You better agree, Conley, or we'll tell a story'll put you in front of a firing squad."

"What kind of story?"

"Like you opened fire on the Rurales without warning. When they only approached for a friendly parley."

"Be your word against mine," Conley said.

"No, Marshal. It'd be the word of *three* of us against yours."

"The word of a lawman against that of convicts."

"A gringo lawman," Fannin said. "And there's a big prejudice against your kind crossing into sovereign Mexico. Dates
back to times when Texas Rangers made a raid or two." He
paused. "That prejudice could damn well outweigh that
nickel-plated star you carry."

Conley thought about this. Fannin could well be right.

Then he asked the question that had bothered him
throughout Fannin's spiel.

"If I did agree to your trade-off," he said, "would you trust
me to live up to my promise? I mean, you hate lawmen, don't
you?"

"Yeah, I hate them," Fannin said. "And I hate your guts as
bad as any, because you've been trying to put me back into
that hellhole." He paused. "But I don't have to like a man to
trust him. At least enough to take a chance."

Conley said, "I think you trust me more than you do the
Mexicans to free you—if they do put me to the wall. You
aren't sure, are you?"

"I ain't sure of anything in this life. Particular down here
in Mexico," Fannin said. "You going to make that promise,
or ain't you?"

"I'll think on it," Conley said.

For the interrogation, Lieutenant Montoya had them all
brought into Conley's cell. The three men, at Montoya's
orders, stood facing him through the bars. Opal he allowed
to sit on a pull-down bunk.

Beside him, in the corridor, were Sergeant Hererra and
the two soldiers, Salas and Juanito.

He was a young officer, but there was a haggard look to
his sensitive features, as if he found his responsibility not
easy to bear. As if he had discovered too late he had chosen
a wrong career.

Conley sensed this, thinking, *Committed, but possibly not
fitted.*

It was a description he had begun, in recent days, to wonder about himself.

"I have heard the stories of my men here," Montoya said, in fluent English, to Conley. "Now I want to hear yours."

Briefly, Conley began to sketch out the story of the prison escape, and his selection to recover the escapees.

"You had no right to enter Mexico without our approval," the lieutenant said.

That was something the prison officials hadn't seemed too concerned about, Conley thought. But he didn't tell the lieutenant that. It would be a surefire way to antagonize him.

Instead, he said, "I had hoped to catch them before they reached the border. And I almost did, at the Tinajas Altas. But they got away and took the Camino del Diablo trail. And I had to follow."

"Still, you had no right," Montoya said.

"Would you want three convicts loose in your area? Desperate people who you don't know what they'd do?"

To his side, Fannin swore. "You son of a bitch!"

"Go on," the lieutenant said. "So you kept on their trail regardless."

"Yes. Then the man the Rurales were after stumbled onto us. Turned out to be an outlaw, too. Friend of Fannin's, here."

"You killed him?"

"By mistake. I thought he was coming for me. He had his gun in hand."

"Then?"

Conley explained about the Quechan slipping away, and how that led to his own capture by the Rurales.

"They were looking to take me in place of the outlaw who I had mistakenly killed. They wanted a victim to take back to the *hacendado* in Hermosillo. And since I was riding the Don's horse, they decided to take me."

He admitted then how he had, in desperation, foolishly told them about the woman.

"You don't know our Rurales too well, it seems," the lieutenant said. He looked angry. "You have heard of rogue horses? We have some rogue police among our Rurales."

"What I did then," Conley said, "I did to save the woman." He gave a detailed description of what followed.

"Unfortunate," the lieutenant said. "Very unfortunate. Especially when you are a marshal of the United States."

He turned to Fannin. "You corroborate his story?"

"No!" Fannin said. "There wasn't any danger to the woman at all. He killed your Rurales because he was afraid they'd take him to Hermosillo. He shot them down in cold blood."

"I see," the lieutenant said. He looked at Pascual, then passed him by. He addressed Opal. "What do you say, *muchacha?* Which one of these is lying?"

She did not answer. Instead, she said, "You have no reason to hold us."

"He killed Rurales," the lieutenant said, gesturing to Conley.

"I mean the rest of us. If you keep him, will you let us go?"

He stared at her for a time without speaking. Then he said, "I wouldn't like to waste provisions on gringo prisoners who haven't broken any Mexican laws."

She was thinking hard about this, he saw.

"Did I answer your question?" he said.

"Tell him!" Fannin said.

She said, "The marshal is telling the truth. I have to say it."

"You bitch!" Fannin said. "You goddamn bitch!"

CHAPTER 11

SEBASTIANO Cos and his band of followers rode into Caborca at a little past noon.

They rode up from the south, and there was no telling what brand of depredation they had been wreaking there, Lieutenant Montoya thought. Usually Cos and his ex-counterrevolutionists roamed the richer pickings of Chihuahua.

Montoya knew of him only by hearsay, and would have preferred that it remained that way.

It was Sergeant Hererra who brought him the news.

"Cos?" Montoya said. "Here?"

"Yes, Lieutenant. They are now watering their mounts at the trough at the edge of the town.

Montoya scowled.

Hererra said, "You know about Cos, Lieutenant?"

"Some," Montoya said. "I know that in his youth he fought with the Lerdo forces against Dìaz. And when Dìaz prevailed, and Lerdo fled to New York City to die in exile, Cos turned into a bandit."*

"He is no longer a youth," Hererra said. "And, God help us, he is said to have turned meaner with age. Once he fought for land reform for the *peones*. Now he pillages to survive."

"How many men with him here?"

"A dozen, I was told. I have not seen them. You understand, sir, I came at once to tell you as soon as I heard."

"Heard in the cantina, I suppose."

*In 1876, Sebastian Lerdo was the president of Mexico, seeking reelection. Porfirio Dìaz led a successful revolt and ruled as a despot until 1911.

124

The sergeant let the comment pass without expression.

"What are your orders, sir?"

"He has a dozen men, you say?"

"So I was told."

"It occurs to you that our garrison is outnumbered?"

"It has occurred to me, yes sir."

"So," the lieutenant said, "we will do nothing now. Perhaps they will eat and drink and ride away. What is there for them here in Caborca?"

"Food, drink, and whores, sir. And a place to raise hell."

"With a garrison of seven men," Montoya said, "I have kept the peace here for several years."

"Yes, sir," Hererra said.

"But we will wait and see what happens," the lieutenant said.

"As you say, sir."

"But stay out of the cantinas. As of now, you are alerted for duty. You and the rest of the roster."

"Yes, sir."

"Stay in garrison. Off the streets. That way I hope to avoid any incidents."

"I have heard, sir, that with Cos and his brigands, there are *always* incidents."

"We will hope we are exceptions," the lieutenant said.

In the cells, Fannin still cursed periodically, although hours had passed since the interrogation. He made it a point to be in a cell corner next to that of Conley when he did so.

Repeatedly, he swore at Opal.

And finally, he said, "She gained nothing for you, Conley. You can see that, can't you? You think that lieutenant will let you go just because you were protecting her from those Rurales?"

"Probably has to give it some thought," Conley said.

"Thought, hell! What's to think about? He knows he can't do it. Whatever those Rurales were, they were legally officers

of the law. Mexican law, Conley. If he let you go, he'd be in
trouble with his superiors."

"So what's your complaint?" Conley said. "If he holds me,
he said he'd turn you loose, if only to save on rations."

"That's what he said, maybe. But I never did trust a Mex.
If he's going to, why ain't he done it?"

The rustler was so frustrated that he was contradicting
himself, Conley thought. He remained silent, and presently
he could hear Fannin on the other side of his cell, again
berating Opal.

Conley mused on what Fannin had said about the lieutenant's not releasing him for fear of censure from above. It
seemed likely to him that Fannin was right.

His own frustration was a match for Fannin's, he thought.
Conley reviewed the actions that had brought about his
predicament, and it didn't ease his feeling any. He had done
what he'd had to do under the circumstances. One damned
thing had led to another.

A dozen years had passed since Sebastiano Cos had been
an idealistic Lerdista colonel, fleeing with a remnant of his
command through Caborca, trying to reach sanctuary in the
United States ahead of a superior force of pursuing Porfistas.

He had barely made it, to save a handful of his men.

Now, at a tired age of thirty-four, he had on a whim
returned to the town from which he had once fled with his
tail between his legs.

In a mind twisted by the intervening years of robbing,
killing, raping, and precarious living, he sought satisfaction
for that other time. This had been the last Mexican town to
witness his debacle. He had sought help here from the
common citizens and been rejected. By then, Lerdisma was
considered a lost cause.

Now, half mad from years of bloodshed, he had decided
to wreak upon the town a measure of his long-deferred
wrath.

He knew some English, and in his mind was an expression the gringos used that described his intentions here: He would "tree the town." It wasn't something new in his repertoire.

It was new only in Caborca.

"What is the temper of the people?" Lieutenant Montoya asked Sergeant Hererra.

The ex-rebels of Sebastiano Cos had been in Caborca for an hour now.

Hererra had received a report during this time from a drinking companion of his among the townsmen.

"My information," Hererra said, "is that thus far the brigands have only drunk, but their mood is growing wilder." He paused. "They have drunk without paying, of course. But no *cantinero* has argued about this. Better to serve them free drinks than to suffer demolition of the cantinas."

"Will they drink and ride on, do you think?"

"Hardly likely, sir. They'll be too drunk to ride, the rate they're going."

"Demolition of the cantinas might be a good thing," Montoya said.

Hererra looked shocked, and said without thinking, "Oh, God no, sir!"

Montoya glared.

"What I meant, sir, is that there is much fear they may shoot up the whole town."

"In which case, how many of our good citizens here will side with us if we confront them?"

"My informant says the people of the town are terrified of the *bandidos*. I would say we would have no volunteers at all. Even my acquaintance has refused to make further reports. He is too afraid he will arouse suspicion on himself."

"Cos is aware, then, of our garrison?"

"Most certainly."

"And our limitations, no doubt?"

"I am sure of it."

"It is likely we can expect an attack, then," Lieutenant Montoya said. "In which case we will be overwhelmed."

"Since we will have no help from the townspeople, yes."

Montoya was silent for a time. Then he said, "Remain on alert. I am going to talk to the prisoners."

"The prisoners, sir?"

"Specifically, to the marshal."

"Yes, sir," Hererra said, watching him walk back to the adjoining guardhouse.

Conley looked up as the lieutenant entered the corridor. He got up from the bunk where he was lying and stepped to the barred front.

He said, "I heard some noise out there on the street a while ago. Some kind of a celebration?"

"Bandits," Montoya said. "Led by a onetime Lerdista rebel. Sebastiano Cos."

"I've heard of him," Conley said. "I thought Chihuahua and Durango were his habitat."

"So did I. Until he rode in an hour ago with a dozen men."

Fannin heard them talking and came to the corner of his and Pascual's cell to listen.

He said, "Cos's *bandidos!* By God! Maybe he'll break us out of this stinking *calabozo* of yours."

"You know him?" Montoya said.

"No, but I'd damn sure like to right about now."

"Don't be too sure of that, *amigo.* He does not like gringos, I've heard."

"What's he got against us?"

"Just being gringos is enough. You have to remember that when he was younger, he fought in Lerdo's revolt against Dìaz. A lot of those former Lerdistas still hate Americans because your country recognized Dìaz as the legitimate head of Mexico's government instead of Lerdo."

Fannin was silent.

"If they should hear you are here, and they will, no doubt,

from the people of the town, they'd more likely break you out to lynch you."

"Then you got to give us guns to protect ourselves."

This time, Montoya remained silent.

Conley said, "Is your garrison strong enough to protect us?"

"I have six men. Cos has a dozen."

"Then Fannin here has a point," Conley said.

"If I gave him a gun, he'd kill you."

"I was thinking of me," Conley said. "I've showed you my credentials as a lawman."

It was some time before Montoya spoke again. Then he said, "Yes, you have shown me. And I have come to believe your story. Yours and that of the woman. We have Rurales who have been known to outrage women." He paused. "If I trusted you with your gun, would you fight Cos's band if they attack the garrison?"

"Would you free me if I did?"

"How can I do that? What explanation could I give?"

"All right," Conley said. "Give me a gun for defense and forget the rest of it. I'll take my chances with a trial court rather than die at the hands of a bunch of gringo-hating brigands."

Fannin said, "If those *bandidos* get to these cells, you and one gun ain't going to save us."

The lieutenant said to Conley, "Give me your word as a marshal of the United States. To use the weapon only against attack by Cos's men. I will free you then to fight beside us. Beyond that I cannot go."

There were shots fired somewhere out on the street.

"Sounds like they're getting wilder," Conley said. "All right, you've got my word."

Fannin said, "What about me? I got a stake in this. And I ain't broke any Mexican laws."

"You are in custody as a material witness against the marshal."

"See where lying gets you?" Conley said.

"Hell, you don't need me," Fannin said. "I admit to lying. Let me go. Or at least give me a gun."

Montoya almost smiled. "I do not think that would be wise. Under the circumstances."

"You are right, there," Conley said.

Fannin's face showed desperation. "What about the girl? You've seemed to sympathize with her on account of those Rurales and all. Well, what about these blood-soaked bastards raising hell out there? They come busting in here, she'll get a working over will make that other look like a church picnic. Give *her* a gun."

"One gun in the hands of the *muchacha* would not stave them off," the lieutenant said.

"She might get one or two," Fannin said. "And a bullet for herself. What I've heard of Cos's bunch, they make old-time Apaches seem civilized."

Montoya turned to Conley. "Marshal?"

"For once I agree with him. Give the girl a fighting chance."

Montoya looked thoughtful. He produced some keys and opened the cell door.

Conley came out.

"Walk ahead of me," Montoya said, motioning down the corridor. "I'll get your gun from my office." As they entered it, he said, "The Indian, he's Quechan, you said? He does not argue one way or another."

"He has learned, I guess, that it does no good where whites are concerned."

"Could you trust him to fight for us?"

"He would fight to protect the woman," Conley said. "He is infatuated with her, I think. Beyond that, I don't know."

"It could be enough. And we need every man we can get."

"You are that certain Cos will attack the garrison?"

There were wild shouts outside, coming from the nearest cantina.

"You hear that?" the lieutenant said. "Those are drunken wild men out there. Men with a long grudge against the government. We can expect the attack." He paused. "The outlaw, Fannin, he is good with a gun?"

Conley said, "Too good. Don't even think about it. His first shot would be at me."

"Yet he has concern for the girl, too, it appears. He asked that she be armed to protect herself."

"That surprised me some. But, then, we men all act strange sometimes when it comes to women," Conley said. He was again thinking of his own feelings about her.

"That is the truth," the young lieutenant said. He seemed to be having similar thoughts from past experiences of his own.

He handed the marshal his gun and belt. "I will take a weapon to the *muchacha*," he said. "But to get back to the Quechan, what do you think?"

"As I said, I think he will fight—to save the girl."

"You would risk him, then?"

It was not a decision Conley found easy to make. Finally, he nodded. "There is a risk," he said. "But I'd take it."

The soldiers were in the anteroom of the sturdy adobe, waiting with nervous expectation. Hererra had them placed at various openings.

Montoya called for Hererra to accompany him and Conley as they returned to the area housing the cells.

Confronting Opal first, he held a pistol through the bars.

"For your defense, *chica*," he said.

She took the weapon.

"You know how to use it?"

"I can shoot," she said. "I grew up on a ranch."

"The bandits of Cos," Montoya said, "they are vicious men." He paused. "You may want to save a bullet for yourself."

She made no answer to that, and after a moment he turned away to the adjacent cell.

"That is the one we can't trust," he said to Hererra, pointing at Fannin. "Against the rear wall, you."

Fannin hesitated.

Hererra scowled and cocked his gun, holding it aimed at Fannin. Fannin moved.

Montoya unlocked the cell, and said to Pascual, "You, Quechan, come out."

Pascual looked at Conley, and Conley said, "You ready to fight to maybe save Opal?"

"I fight for her," Pascual said.

"Come out, then. But no funny business, understand?"

Pascual came out, saying nothing.

"Goddammit!" Fannin said. "Let me out too. I can shoot rings around that Injun."

For answer, Montoya locked the cell door.

"You sons of bitches!" Fannin said.

The garrison had been built back when the Apaches had sometimes made raids down this way.

It had been, therefore, designed as something of a fort, with narrow window openings in its heavy walls. At these, now, the soldiers waited, tensely expectant at those facing the street.

"You expecting a frontal assault, Lieutenant?" Conley said.

"In the beginning, at least. They are drunk and filled with liquor courage. And Cos's kind are reckless of life when they do battle, I have heard. Life is cheap to them, as it is to all who do much killing."

Back in the adjoining cell corners, Fannin said to Opal, whom he could not see, "Listen, sweetheart, if you want to save yourself, you'd best turn that gun over to me."

"I know how to use it," she said. "My father taught me how when I was just a kid."

"He teach you how to kill a man? It's some different from shooting at tin cans."

"You squeeze the trigger the same way," she said.

"That's the easy part," Fannin said. "The hard part, for somebody like you, is not to panic when a live body is coming at you. A live body made of flesh and blood, just like you."

"I can do it."

"I could do it for you better."

"If I'm attacked in here, you couldn't even see it."

"I could shoot the bastards before they got in there."

"How many? No, I'll take my own chances." She paused. "You only want the gun to defend yourself."

He said sullenly then, "You're as mule-minded as tht marshal friend of yours. The two of you could make a team."

His words took her mind off her predicament for a moment.

In the interior front of the garrison, the soldiers peered cautiously through the narrow windows to survey the street. Across it and two doors down was the cantina from which most of the noise emanated.

The street at this moment was clear.

Conley and Pascual stood aside with Montoya. From time to time Conley studied Pascual, and Montoya studied both of them.

The Quechan did not meet the stare of either. He stood with his eyes roving the room, from window to window to the heavy wood door.

Seeing that, Conley worried about his intentions. He met the eyes of the lieutenant and saw his own doubt reflected there.

From the window opening nearest the door, Sergeant Hererra said, "They are coming out of the cantina, Lieutenant."

Montoya and Conley each moved to an opening to see for himself.

"The one with the red mustache," Hererra said, "that will be Cos."

"The one still standing in the cantina doorway?" Conley said.

"He was once a colonel," the sergeant said. "He'll risk his men, not himself, most likely."

The words seemed to sting the lieutenant, and he said, "That is a colonel's job, Sergeant."

Hererra said hastily, "I meant no offense, sir."

As he finished his comment, a bullet was fired. It came through the opening and struck him in the forehead. He fell back, striking Pascual.

Pascual jerked away as the corpse landed at his feet.

And then shots came in a rush, fired with drunken abandonment.

Bullets whipped past the defenders as they ducked beneath the windowsills. The lead slammed into the opposite walls, chipping chunks from the adobe.

The soldiers at the windows thrust weapons forth and fired. They were at once driven to crouches again as a fusillade filled the openings.

And now the attackers were up close to the exterior, and hidden from sight of the defenders.

Almost at once there was a pounding on the door, and then the battering of live bodies thrown recklessly against it.

The door held.

Shots followed, blasting away at the heavy latch.

The latch held, but the heavy slugs splintered the wood around it.

"Stay at the windows!" Montoya yelled. "Let no one reach in!"

His men were doing that, and as the attackers shoved guns to fire into the room, the defenders fired out, catching them point-blank, eliciting their screams.

The door was now the danger spot, Conley thought, and he fell back, as did Pascual and the lieutenant. They aimed their weapons at the door and waited.

A burst of shots literally cut the latch from the wood, and the door swung on its hinges.

One of Cos's men burst through and met bullets fired by the waiting three.

Behind him came another, trampling over his body. Conley shot him.

At one window, Salas, caught with excitement, leaned into an opening, trying to search out a bandit he had glimpsed a second before.

The bandit partly reappeared, and put a bullet in his heart before he could shoot. Salas died as he hit the floor.

Another bandit, rushing over his crumpled comrades in the doorway, caught a second fusillade from Conley and Pascual.

Montoya took a bullet in an exchange with one more reckless attacker before the bandit went down. It struck him in the shoulder, spun him around to slam him up against the rear wall, where he remained standing, gun at the ready.

But with four men piled dead in the doorway, the brigands were sobering enough to realize a need for different strategy.

Montoya was gushing blood from his wound. His face was pale.

He said to Conley, "We're still outnumbered."

Conley said, "Where's Cos?"

The lieutenant had moved to one side of the doorway, trying to see the front of the cantina, trying to see if Cos was still there.

"Not in sight."

"Would he lose men like this and do nothing?"

"Not Cos," Montoya said. "Whatever he is, he has big balls."

"Then what is he up to?"

"I wish I knew," the lieutenant said.

"The cells," Conley said. "Is there another way in?"

"None. You have to come through here to get to them."

The firing from the street was more sporadic now.

"Would Cos know that?" Conley said.

"I doubt it. He probably knows by now there are gringos there, is all."

Even as he spoke, the explosion came.

"Dynamite!" Conley said.

"The corridor wall, by the sound!"

"Somebody told him the layout," Conley said. He made a rush for the rear.

He heard Pascual at his heels.

The corridor was a shambles.

But already three bandits had crawled in through the gaping hole.

Conley's first thought was of Opal, but the three ignored the cells. They were coming fast toward the garrison office, two side-by-side with guns in hand, one leading.

The one in the lead had a red mustache.

He was six paces away when he saw Conley just beyond the doorway.

Cos's gun came up just as Conley fired.

Conley's bullet caught him in the belly, and as he folded over, Conley and Pascual fired over him, by bad luck each targeting the same one of the trailing pair.

The one not hit shot wildly, but his slug caught Pascual in the face, dropping him dead.

Conley pumped two shots into his chest.

And Cos, from where he had lain unmoving, came to life and lifted himself to aim his gun at Conley.

"Gringo bastard!" he said.

Conley squeezed his trigger and heard the gun click empty.

And from the far end of the corridor, Opal, cheek pressed against her cell bars, arm awkwardly thrust out, fired a chancy shot that took Cos in the spine, killing him.

The following morning, the dead were buried.

Those of Cos's band who survived had galloped away as

soon as they learned that Cos was dead. They rode east toward the Sierra Madre.

"Back to Chihuahua, we hope," Lieutenant Montoya said. "Back where their luck has been better."

He was standing in front of the garrison stables. His wound had been treated by the local medico, and his left arm was in a sling.

Conley was mounted, as was Opal beside him. Fannin was mounted, too, manacles again on his wrists. The pack animals had been freshly provisioned from the garrison stores.

Conley had his weapons back.

Lieutenant Montoya said, "I will send word to Hermosillo that the three Rurales died bravely in our defense against Cos's marauders. The prized horse of Don Luis will be returned to him, by whoever he sends to retrieve it. Don Luis will also be glad to hear that the three Rurales killed the horse thief while reclaiming the horse."

The two men searched each other's face for a considerable time. Then the lieutenant said, "You understand? This is for what you did here, for me and for Caborca."

"I understand," Conley said.

"Then take your prisoners and go with luck," the lieutenant said.

CHAPTER 12

THEY took the main road northward toward Sonoita.

Conley wanted to get out of Mexico as quickly as possible. He had encountered enough trouble down here. His desire now was to avoid any more contact with Mexicans, be they Rural Police, army, or brigands.

Once, when they rested briefly, he said, "When we cross the border, we can relax some."

He was speaking to Opal, but it was Fannin who answered.

"*You* can, maybe," Fannin said. "But all we see ahead is that prison getting closer and closer."

"Yeah," Conley said. "I suppose."

"You suppose," Fannin said. "But you don't *know*. Nobody can know who's never been there."

Conley had no answer for that.

"Chrissakes, man, don't you have no human feeling? I mean after all we been through together, fighting off Cos's bunch and all."

"I don't recall you had a part in that."

"That wasn't my fault. I wanted to fight."

Maybe he did, Conley thought.

Fannin said, "By God! You ought to remember what the girl did for you. She saved your life."

"I recollect that," Conley said.

"Well?"

"Well, what?"

"Jesus!" Fannin said.

"What's that mean?"

"What the hell kind of a man are you? Don't you figure you owe her for that?"

138

Opal had been listening without looking at either man. But now she turned to study Conley's face.

After a moment, he said, "I reckon I do."

"*Reckon* you do? By God, Marshal, you are one of a kind! I've seen some hard-nosed lawmen, but they weren't even in the contest, comes to you."

Conley said, "A man is what he is."

"Jesus!" Fannin repeated with disbelief and disgust.

On the afternoon of the third day, they reached the town, three miles south of the border. Sonoita was a clutch of adobe huts, with plots of corn and grain and vegetables surrounding, a pretty good sign that there was well water available.

And water they were ready for.

There was a single cantina at the intersection of two dirt roadways. At this hour of the day, the streets were empty. At a hitch rack in front of the cantina a blue-eyed, dappled gray gelding was tied.

As they rode by on their way to a water trough a few doors down, Fannin gave the horse a hard study. Then, abruptly, he faced forward and did not look backward again.

Conley noted that, and threw a second glance himself at the tethered mount. A china-eyed horse was a rarity in any man's country, he was thinking. He could understand Fannin's interest being caught by it.

Opal had noticed it too.

They watered the stock, drank themselves from a pipe leading from a nearby tank, and Conley refilled the canteens and water bags.

Fannin, dismounted, stood to one side, hands still cuffed:

"Dammit, Marshal, I could sure go for a drink."

"You just had one," Conley said.

"Not water. I mean a real drink, there at the cantina."

The same thought had been in Conley's mind. He pondered it again.

Fannin said, "After what we been through lately, have a heart for a change."

"Can't take the girl into a saloon," Conley said.

"You forgetting what she is? She ain't no schoolmarm, she's a convict."

Conley was silent.

"And that ain't a saloon," Fannin said. "It's a *cantina,* and they got different customs. They tolerate women in them."

"Go ahead, Marshal," Opal said. "I'll wait here with the livestock. I never had a taste for liquor."

"But can I trust you?"

Fannin said, "You ask that? After she saved your life in that shoot-out?"

"All right," Conley said. "Just one drink. Or maybe two."

"First time I ever saw you act human," Fannin said. "How about taking off the cuffs before we go in?"

"You can raise a glass two-handed as well as one."

"I take back what I just said."

"You want that drink or don't you?"

"I want it," Fannin said.

They led the horses and the pack stock back to the cantina rack, and tied them next to the dappled gray.

"Won't be more than five minutes," Conley said to Opal. "You have any trouble out here, you holler."

She nodded.

"Come on," he said to Fannin. "Walk in first."

They approached the single wide door, which was open.

After the bright sunlight, the interior was half dark. Conley cursed to himself as he stepped in behind Fannin. It was a sucker move, going in that way. Anything could have happened.

He got his eyes focused and saw the crude bar was empty except for a pair of Mexicans in *peon*-white cottons at the far end and a gringo in range clothes at the end nearest the door.

They all stared at him, then at the manacles worn by Fannin, then back at him.

Fannin went to stand at the bar. He turned so he was facing the gringo cowboy a few feet away. They exchanged stares.

Conley said to Fannin, "Order what you want."

"Whiskey," Fannin said to the thin Mexican bartender. He did not take his eyes from the gringo.

The bartender said, "Chure. I got good *yanqui* whiskey here."

"The same for me, then," Conley said.

The bartender set out two glasses and poured from an unlabeled bottle. When Fannin lifted his drink with both hands, the bartender pretended not to notice.

Fannin downed it in one gulp.

Conley tasted his, then tossed it off. He said to the barman, "How far to the town of Ajo?"

"Forty mile, *señor.*"

"Give us another," Conley said.

"Chure," the Mexican said. He refilled their glasses.

Conley looked to the end of the bar where the *peons* were. They had stopped looking at him. They kept their eyes now on the beer in the glasses in front of them.

He looked to the end of the bar where the gringo rider was, and the man looked away too.

Fannin called to him, "That china-eyed horse outside yours?"

"Yeah." The rider studied the manacles again, and the convict clothes. "Don't look like you're in a position to steal him."

Fannin said, "Just trying to be friendly. My name is Fannin. Sam Fannin. You got any friends around these parts, you might tell them you met me."

"You expect me to say, 'pleased to meet you'?"

"Enough talk," Conley said. "Drink up and let's go."

"Sure," Fannin said.

Opal looked impatient when Coley and Fannin returned.

"I started to worry," she said, "that somebody might try to steal the horses. This is a very poor-looking town."

"I knew you'd watch them well," Conley said.

"Yeah, I did. I'd hate to walk from here to Gila Bend."

They untied the animals, and Conley gave the china-eyed gray another look. "Now, that's a horse. You see him once, you won't soon forget him."

Fannin said nothing.

In a few minutes, they were on the road north toward Ajo.

In the cantina, the gringo rider paid the Mexican bartender for a final drink.

"You gonna go to Ajo, Slade?" the barman said.

"I got business there," Slade said. "Why?"

He was a lean-bodied man with a weathered face. The Mexican could not tell how old Slade was.

"I just ask," the Mexican said.

"You ought to know not to ask by now," Slade said.

"Chure I know, Slade. You try to get to Ajo ahead of them people?"

"Goddammit!" Slade said. "There ain't nothing worse than a nosy Mexican."

"I was just ask," the barman said.

As dusk came, they turned off the Ajo road to make camp.

Later, when they spread blankets, Conley again trussed Fannin, but left Opal free.

He spread her blanket close to his. He could hear her tired breathing, and thought she was asleep. He was startled when she spoke.

"Will we be in Ajo tomorrow?"

"Should be, with no trouble," he said.

"They have a hotel where I might get a bath?"

"We'll see."

"What about Fannin?"

"I recall there's a jail there to keep him overnight."

"Deputy sheriff, too, I suppose."

"Town marshal. Nearest deputy is at Gila."

"You got the price of a bath for me?"

"Yeah."

"Promise?"

"Yeah." He was conscious more than ever of her lying only a few feet away.

"I'd sure appreciate it, Marshal."

He did not speak for a minute. Then he said, gruffly, "Get some sleep."

She thought, *When I said that, it bothered him.*

She lay awake for a while, thinking about this.

Once she heard a horse out on the road, heading north.

For some reason it reminded her of that china-eyed dapple gray they'd seen hitched at the cantina back in Sonoita.

She didn't know why.

Ajo was a cluster of mining-town structures sprawled on a flat valley surrounded by low peaks from which copper had been extracted for more than a hundred years, first by the Spaniards.

For thirty-four years now it had been pretty much run by the Ajo Copper Company.

That's about all Conley knew about it.

There were plenty of off-shift miners walking the dirt streets.

As they entered the outskirts, he hailed one of them. The man stopped and stared at him, the horses and pack stock, and then appraised the man and woman in convict garb.

Conley had pinned his lawman's star in sight since leaving Mexico, and the miner's glance came to rest on that.

"Looking for the jail?" he said.

"Yeah."

"Must be a stranger here."

"Here once, a long time ago," Conley said. "Deputy U.S. marshal, out of Florence."

"Three blocks ahead, then turn right two," the miner said. "The jail is right across from the bank."

"Obliged," Conley said. "I recall it now."

"Them's convicts you got there? They escape from jail?"

"Prison."

"I never seen a woman convict before," the miner said. "They any different from the men?"

Conley ignored the question, kicked his mount, and got his train moving.

The miner stood staring after them. "What the hell got into him?" he said.

Conley herded his little procession along the directions given.

As he turned right and rode into the second block where the jail was, he could see two guards with holstered guns emerge from a stagecoach in front of the bank. They were carrying a strongbox between them.

A shotgun guard had just jumped down from beside the driver, and stood between the coach and the bank with his weapon held waist high.

It was a sight Conley had witnessed more than once over the years, and its significance registered at once.

Payroll delivery, he thought. For the mines. Must have come in from Gila Bend.

From fifty yards away he saw the guards with the box step toward the bank entrance, and then he heard the shots.

The guards carrying the box fell, dropping it, even as the one with the shotgun went down, firing a futile blast into the sky.

The driver of the stage snapped his reins, and the startled team jerked it into a lurch to escape.

From across the street, three riders raced to the bank front. Two dismounted, and while one held the reins of both horses, the other bent to grab the strongbox and heave it up to the third.

He balanced it across his mount's withers, whirled as the

others remounted, and all came racing toward Conley. The two unencumbered with the box had their guns in hand.

Even as he drew his own gun, Conley recognized one of them as the stranger from Sonoita, riding now a bay in place of the china-eyed gray.

No surprise showed on the man's face, and with his pistol already fisted, he beat Conley's shot. His bullet caught Conley's horse in the neck. The horse pitched violently, and Conley lost his grip on his gun.

Two more riders came racing from the jail front, standbys during the robbery. One of them fired at Conley as he slipped to the ground to retrieve his weapon from the dust.

The rider missed, but swerved his horse to knock Conley sprawling.

Just beyond, the rider from Sonoita reached Fannin and said, "Let's go, Sam. You got here damn near too late. We couldn't wait. Had the payroll to tend to."

"Yeah," Fannin said. "But I knew you'd try to spring me."

He swung his mount up against Opal's. She was fighting it as it pitched, excited by the shooting. He reached out and grabbed the reins and jerked them from her hands.

A moment later, he was racing off behind Slade.

The rider who'd bowled Conley over had got hold of the lead rope of the pack mule, and then they were thundering away to the south, five bank robbers, Fannin, and the girl.

In the confusion, Conley's mount had run away eastward down the street and disappeared.

People poured out of the bank and were staring at Conley as he got to his feet. He stared back.

And then they were running across the street toward the jail, to bunch up around a body lying there.

Conley caught up the burro's lead and started toward them.

One of them, dressed as a businessman, eyed his star.

A man lay dead inside the group.

He, too, wore a badge.

"Bastards, shot him down, cold-blooded, as he came out his office," the townsman said.

"Town marshal?"

"Yeah. Selah Riley. Only been hired a few months back. Know him?"

Conley shook his head.

"I'm Warren Woodruff, mine manager. Ajo Copper Company owns the bank. That was the monthly payroll they took. Eighteen thousand dollars."

"Mining company owns the bank?" Conley said.

"Ajo Copper owns the town." Woodruff paused, then said, "And we want that money back."

Conley's mind was working, only half listening. He was thinking about Fannin and the girl getting away.

"You better get a posse together fast," Woodruff said.

"What?" Conley said.

"You're a U.S. marshal, aren't you? And with Selah dead, it's up to you. Your kind of job more than his, anyway. What's your name?"

"Conley. Ridge Conley."

"Seems I heard that name before."

A bystander next to Woodruff said, "Me, too." He paused, then said to Conley, "Ain't you the lawman they sent to get them escaped convicts back?"

"Yeah."

"I read it in the Gila newspaper a few days back. But what're you doing here?"

"Bringing them in."

"The girl and the man that just rode off with them hard cases?"

Conley nodded but did not answer. It was a sore point with him just to think about.

"I'll draft some posse volunteers for you, Marshal," Woodruff said. "And get you a guide that knows the country around here. Though the holdup bunch headed south. For Mexico, I'd guess."

Mexico! Conley thought. Again?

He said, "My horse took a bullet, went running off."

"We'll get you one. The men, too. Let's waste no more time. I want you on the trail in twenty minutes!"

The man's tone irritated Conley, but he did not object. He was eager to get after his two lost captives. As impatient as Woodruff himself.

Three-quarters of an hour later he was heading a posse of ten men out of town. Beside him rode a former prospector who Woodruff claimed knew this part of Arizona if anybody did.

That was just in case those wild bastards hadn't struck for the border.

Conley was hoping to hell they hadn't. He'd had his fill of Sonora for a while.

A short distance south of Ajo, the grizzled ex-prospector, known familiarly to the posse as Jason, halted at a faint trail leading west.

He quickly pointed out that a hurried attempt had been made here to brush out the hoofprints of several riders. He walked with Conley a few paces along the trace to where the futile erasures ended.

"That's them, Marshal."

"What lies in that direction?" Conley said.

"Rough country. Hundred miles of uninhabited desert, with rugged mountain ranges running north and south through it."

"Uninhabited, you say?"

"Except maybe for some damn fool prospector like I used to be. Or some owlhooters looking for a quick place to lose a posse."

Conley stared into the distance ahead. The first range was turning purplish as the sunlight passed beyond it.

"That's the Growler Range," Jason said. "They could hole up there tonight."

"We'll push on, then, long as we can see their trail."

"My thought exactly," Jason said. "If we don't catch up to them there, we'll have a job of work on our hands."

As they returned to the waiting riders, Jason said, "I ain't got it straight in my head about them convicts you were herding. Seems like that holdup gang was acquainted with them."

"Some knew the male convict, I guess," Conley said. "The one took the first shot at me had words with him down in Sonoita. Not particularly friendly words, so I thought nothing of it. But they must have been old acquaintances."

"Looks like you came into town at exactly the wrong time, Marshal. For your sake, I mean."

"Looks like it."

"Good for us, though, to have a badge along," Jason said. "Lends authority to a posse. In case of a lynching."

"Lynching?"

Jason gave him a sly smile. "Most of these boys riding with us is company miners. That stole money was for their wages. They aint't likely to take kindly to them that took it."

Conley said, "My convicts had no part in the robbery."

Jason showed surprise. "Sounds like you taken a liking for them," he said. "Or maybe just the lady, hey?"

"Nothing like that," Conley said.

"She's a good-looking wench, you get her cleaned up, I'll bet," Jason said.

Conley thought, *She never got a chance to take that bath.*

He said, "That's got nothing to do with it."

"I didn't mean no offense, Marshal."

"None taken," Conley said.

He was thinking now of how to prevent a possible lynching. Hell, he thought, they wouldn't lynch a woman. Or would they?

Darkness stopped them as they could no longer see the outlaws' tracks on the trail. The Growlers were close now, but they could not be sure the robbers had gone into them. If they'd turned off, it would just be time wasted to continue.

They made a dry camp and spread their blankets, and Conley aroused them at first light.

The tracks did go straight west, but not for long. Presently, Jason spotted where they turned southwesterly into a rocky dry wash.

Jason said, "Trail sign will be harder to come by now. Ain't no trail, really. Looks to me like they're trying to skirt around the Growlers, instead of climbing into them."

"Any water holes where they're heading?"

"Only if you know where to find them," Jason said. "We got canteens with us. Did they?"

"I recall they did. And they took my pack mule. Couple of water bags there, part full, and some provisions left. Not enough, unless they had supplies in their saddlebags."

"If they smart enough to plan a bank robbery, they probably did," Jason said.

"I guess."

"I know the country here as well as anybody," Jason said. "But I ain't familiar with outlaw thinking. Now, with you being a marshal, you probably are. What do you think will be their intentions?"

"I'd guess they hope to shake off any pursuit," Conley said, "and then strike out for towns somewhere. Most likely split up. Divide the payroll. Pick different destinations."

"They come into a hell of an area to do it," Jason said.

"For us, or for them?" Conley said.

"For both of us. You go roaming around one of these deserts this time of year, it ain't no picnic ground."

"Tell me about it," Conley said. "As if I didn't know."

CHAPTER 13

THEY continued along the wash. To their right was a high escarpment of the Growlers, to their left a lesser one, but which still cut off their sight in that direction.

The rocky surface of the wash narrowed. There was sand here, too, which yielded plenty of hoofprints.

The prints weren't needed; there was only one way through. The sun was high enough now to turn the canyon into a furnace, and it was only midmorning.

The canyon floor had been rising as they rode, but now it came to a leveling off to a flat summit.

"Odd contour," Conley said.

"Yeah," Jason said. "Sort of a split watershed, ain't it? Look up ahead, and you'll see where it starts going down."

"Watershed," Conley said. "What water?"

"You been around the Territory enough to know what flash floods can do."

"What little rain falls here," Conley said, "it must have taken a thousand years."

"Easy that," Jason said. He rode in silence, then said, "It'll take us down into a desert basin between the Growlers here and the next range."

More than an hour passed, and then the canyon widened into a shallow wash such as they had entered on the eastern side earlier.

On this side there was sign of ancient volcanic eruptions, spewings of lava boulders, and glimpses of half-buried black basaltic flows, arrested as they had once cooled.

In the noon heat it was hard to believe anything had ever

cooled, Conley thought. They huddled in misery for a brief break, and he appraised the condition of the posse.

Jason appeared to be taking it all in stride. He looked a hell of a lot better than Conley felt.

The miners, though, were suffering. They were out of their element, he thought. And none of them were riders to start with. Already he could see their disenchantment with the pursuit.

It was nearly always the same. He had led civilian posses before, and after the initial excitement wore off, a quick waning of interest usually set in.

That even happened when the members were range men. And with townsmen, or even hardworking miners such as these, it was worse.

Well, he hadn't picked the men, Woodruff had. And time had been a critical element in forming the bunch.

He wondered how long some of them would last if the chase was long. It could depend largely on their anger at having their payroll solen, delaying their pay. Unpredictable, he thought.

Some of them groaned as they mounted, and he took that as a bad sign. The best he could hope for was a short chase.

And a successful gunfight.

A couple of miles later, they came out into the basin. In the distance they could see the far outline of the next mountains.

"The Granite Range," Jason said.

"You suppose they're headed there?"

"We'll soon know," Jason said. "But they damn sure ain't going to stay out there on the flats. No water, no game. No nothing."

Opal wasn't at all sure she wanted to be with them.

Had not Fannin, even manacled, seized her reins and dragged her along as they fled from Ajo, she was almost certain she would have stayed behind.

And why had he done it?

She had never been sure of what kind of man he was. The one word that seemed to describe him told her nothing. Contradictory, that's what he was. A man of fleeting changes of impulse that seemed to reflect a war within himself.

Rustler, hard case, killer, he was all of those.

And yet there were rare times when he showed a sensitive side toward her. She could recall his sharing the water of his canteen in the early stages of their escape. There were other incidents that came to her mind.

She thought of his being responsible for the Mexican lieutenant's giving her a gun to protect herself. That had been at Fannin's urging. It turned out he'd had an ulterior motive, but was that exclusively the reason? Might he really have been concerned for what could happen to her?

He had made some crude remarks occasionally, but never had he tried to force himself upon her. She sensed he was a virile male and that he must have a normal lust for women. Thinking of it now, she felt surprise that he had kept it under control.

So why had he dragged her with him?

Was it because he knew of her dread of being imprisoned and sought to give her another chance at freedom? That could be it, but, if so, it showed a depth of empathy she would not have expected from him.

The previous night, which they had spent in the rocky wash, she had lain a few feet from him, fearful of him, but still more fearful of the others.

He had told her, briefly, that the one called Slade had been in the cantina at Sonoita. She had gathered there was an earlier favor owed him by Slade, and that he had let Slade know he could use repayment. It was Slade who had used rocks to free his manacles.

"It was pretty much chance, though," he'd told her, "that we blundered into that holdup at the right time."

"Your *friends*," she said, giving heavy emphasis to the word, "where are they running to?"

"Soon as we get through this canyon, they'll be turning south. Cutting through the range like this, they hope to throw off any posse might come after us."

"South?"

"Little border town of Quitobaquito," Fannin said. "Back into Sonora."

"Oh, my God!" she said. "Not again!"

"You don't like the idea?"

"Of course I don't! Do you?"

He did not answer at once. Then he said, "I been thinking of another way."

"Where?"

"North."

"Why?"

He looked at her thoughtfully before he said, "East is Ajo. We can't go back there. South is Mexico. West is nothing but desert and mountains for a hundred miles, and beyond is Yuma. So that leaves north."

"North to where?"

"The railroad. Maybe we can ride the boxcars east. Ain't likely they'd be looking for us up there after this length of time. I'm thinking New Mexico would be a place to go. I rustled cows there a few years back."

"What about me?" she said.

"You'll have a choice," he said. "You can stick with me, or you can cut loose on your own."

She stared at him, and he stared back.

He said then, "You know what I am, I guess, by now. But I ain't all bad." He paused. "I never had a steady woman of my own. If you found it suitable, I'd admire for you to be her."

When she looked shocked, he said, "Didn't you know I wanted you—from the beginning?"

She said, finally, "No. Not from the beginning."

"Now you know," he said. He paused. "Come with me now. I won't hurt you. Later, you can decide the rest."

She almost said, *I don't have much choice,* but she didn't. For the first time, she felt she didn't want to hurt him.

"I'll go," she said. She was far less afraid of him now than she was of his bank-robbing companions.

Not that she was totally without fear. He was a man of quick, flaring moods, she thought. He had to be handled like a charge of dynamite set to go off.

Jason pointed out the trail sign, there on the desert's edge, just west of the Growler Range.

"There it is, Marshal. A split-up. The wild bunch going south and taking your pack mule with them. The convict and the girl riding north."

The hoofprints of the latter were recognizable enough to Conley. He'd been riding behind them all the way from Caborca.

One of the posse, a big man with a miner's muscles rippling beneath his sweat-soaked shirt, said grumpily, "The hell with them two. That payroll is what we been sent to get."

Jason was studying Conley's face. "Marshal?" he said.

"You know the answer," Conley said. "My priority is to get those escapees back."

The big miner said, "Woodruff put you in charge of running them robbers down. And Woodruff speaks for the Ajo Copper Company. You better think twice what you do now. The company swings a lot of weight in Territory politics."

"You've got enough men to handle them," Conley said.

"If we catch them."

"Jason can track them."

"And after we catch them, if we do? Ain't none of us ever run up against a bunch of desperadoes. We been relying on that badge and six-gun of yours to tilt the odds in a showdown. And hell, Jason ain't no more gunfighter than I am. Neither are the rest."

"Well, Marshal?" Jason said.

The big man said, "You leave us now, and Ajo Copper is going to be your enemy for life."

"He's telling it true there," Jason said.

"I won't argue that," Conley said. "So I guess I've just added another enemy to my list."

Fannin tried to talk Slade out of the pack mule with its few remaining supplies.

"No way," Slade said.

"You've got jerky, beans, and bacon in your saddlebags," Fannin said. "The girl and I got nothing."

"Tough," Slade said. "I had my way, we'd keep the girl with us. Once we're clear of any pursuit, she'd come in handy for sport."

"I done you a favor once," Fannin said.

"Sure you did," Slade said. "And I done you one, busting you loose from that lawman was dragging you back to the pen."

"Keep the pack mule, then. Just give us enough to last us till we reach the railroad."

"Might be we can do that," Slade said. "Let me talk to the boys."

"And a rifle, maybe, in case we got to hunt," Fannin said.

Slade nodded.

He went from one to another of the men. After some discussion, he went to the pack on the mule and opened it up. He motioned to Fannin and rationed him out a meager amount of what was left of the supplies.

Fannin took them without comment, putting some in the saddlebags of each of his and Opal's mounts.

"Ain't much," Slade said. "But you ought to reach the railroad in forty, fifty miles."

"Yeah," Fannin said.

"I figure this puts me one up on you now, when it comes to who owes who," Slade said.

"Yeah, sure," Fannin said. "But if you could spare a little cash for when we get there, I'd be even more beholden."

"We split the take last night," Slade said, "between the five of us."

"I saw."

"Come to about three and a half thousand each. Sure beats hell out of rustling as a way to make a living."

"Maybe you can spare train fare to Lordsburg for me and the girl, then."

"How much?"

"Been a while since I rode a train."

Slade reached into a pocket and took out some bills and leafed through them. "Here's fifty."

"I won't forget it."

"Hope it keeps you out of the pen," Slade said.

Conley watched the posse of miners ride south, led by Jason.

It had to be that way, he thought, although it wasn't all to his liking.

As a lawman his inclination was to be with them, or, more exactly, to be on the trail of those who had perpetrated the bank crime.

Stacked against this inclination was the greater one to recapture Fannin and Opal.

And besides this were the other opposing concerns: that the inexperienced possemen might be annihilated by the hardcase bunch if they did catch up to them, and his more urgent one over Opal's welfare, now that she was alone in the control of Fannin.

Fannin, he thought. Even after the many days on the trail with the truculent rustler, he had ambivalent feelings about him.

As near as he could sum up, his appraisal of the man was: *He's not as bad as some I've known.*

Which wasn't saying a hell of a lot.

And which wasn't going to have a bearing on what he, Conley, had to do.

And that was to capture him again before he got out of the area and disappeared into the vast territory beyond.

With Opal.

Their trail skirted the edge of the desert where it abutted the foothills of the Growlers. At this point it veered slightly westward.

Fannin was not wasting time trying to hide direction, Conley thought. It was obvious he was interested mostly on holding any lead he had on a possible pursuer.

Conley could visualize his scanning the backtrail, wondering if they were being followed.

That led to the thought that the lead might be less than the hoofprints indicated. Conley guessed that he might be no more than an hour behind. In the desert heat, horse droppings dried within minutes, so the manure could give no accurate reading of when the animals passed.

Fannin might even be so near as to have seen him following.

With that in mind, Conley kept peering ahead, weighing sites of likely ambush in the confused strewing of cholla, ocotillo, occasional saguaros, and rocky outcrops.

In the distance he could see the dipped outline of what could be a pass between the range and another beyond.

He dug out his map again. It was now faded from sweat and use, and hard to read. And the shown contours did not seem to conform exactly to the actual terrain, but he laid this to the vagaries of mapmaking.

Once through the pass, due north ten or fifteen miles should put the convicts into the Crater Mountains, he decided. And beyond that into a flat desert all the way to the railroad.

If that was where they were headed.

It was a likely destination, he thought. The railroad could mean a way east, a way out of the Territory. And possible freedom from Arizona law.

At that moment he set himself a goal. *I have got to catch them before they reach the railroad,* he thought.

They reached the pass, and from its summit Fannin spent the period of resting horses by scrutinizing the flat country they had left.

He did this in silence, absorbed, as a quarter of an hour went by.

Opal said finally, "Well, what are you seeing?"

"Nothing," he said. "You can see how thick the haze is. I can't see any sign of anybody."

"We never did know if there was a posse out," she said. "And if there was, they'd be after the bank robbers, not us."

"True enough," he said. "Unless the marshal was with them."

"They'd still go after those with the payroll."

"Use your head, girl. If Conley was with them, he'd take our trail. That's his job."

"Alone?"

"Of course alone. Ain't that been what he's done ever since we busted out?"

"Yes, you're right. But if you can't see him, he must be pretty far behind."

"I doubt it. But there's no telling, in that haze out there. He could be as close as the canyon below."

"Sometimes I think we should give up. Go back and serve our time."

"The sun making you crazy?" he said. "There'll be years added on now for escaping."

"How many?"

"A couple, at least. Maybe five. Maybe more, I don't know."

"Five!" she said. "Oh, God!"

"Yeah," he said. "You keep that in mind, girl, and you won't even consider giving up."

"I couldn't stand it. I'd die."

"Sure you would," Fannin said. "And don't you forget it." He paused. "It'll keep you in mind of who your friend is. Me."

"I do appreciate what you're doing. Now."

"Different than it was, ain't it?"

"I guess I wasn't thinking about added-on time," she said. "Conley never mentioned it."

"Of course he didn't. Whatever he is, he ain't stupid. He'd know it would rile you up."

"I think he just didn't want me to feel worse than I did," she said. "He never treated me badly."

Fannin scowled. "Neither did I."

"I guess not."

"You guess?"

"I guess," she said again.

He shrugged. "Well, that's better than nothing. It'll have to do for now."

She was instantly suspicious. "What do you mean, 'for now'?"

He shrugged again, and was silent. Then he said, "Mount up. We better keep moving."

"You *do* think he's back there," she said. "Close?"

"I know he is," he said. "None of Slade or the others could remember shooting him. One of them remembered hitting his horse, is all."

Oddly, his words made her feel better.

She got into the saddle, then said, "Do you know the country up ahead?"

"Never been in it. But going north, we can't help but hit the railroad." Suddenly, he grinned. "Someplace between Gila Bend and Yuma."

"Not Yuma!"

"You keep feeling that way, girl, and we'll be all right. You just stick to Sam Fannin, and he'll look after you. You keep that in mind."

What choice do I have? she thought.

Even if we reach the railroad, what choice will *I have?*

And if I go east with him into New Mexico, will he expect me to stick with him, even then?

Conley reached the pass before sighting the couple. The haze that had formed along the desert edge of the Growlers had prevented this before.

Now, looking northward, he could see them crossing the plain that reached toward the Crater Range.

Two tiny dark figures plodding across another rugged basin. He judged them to be halfway.

By the time he reached their present position, they would have reached the Craters, he judged.

If he was to catch up, he'd have to press on, hoping they'd camp, or at least rest, once in the mountains. Luckily, Woodruff, the Ajo Copper Company manager, had given him a strong, rested, mount. And those ridden by Fannin and Opal had been on the trail ever since they'd left Caborca.

He had never been in the Craters, and he wondered if Fannin had. That could make a difference, he knew. Was there timber in the high reaches that could provide hiding for him and the girl?

From here, at this time of day, all he could see was a mass of dun-colored slopes and shadowed contours. There must be water there, though.

If you knew where to find it.

He had used his canteen sparingly, just in case, because of that other desert north of the Craters, stretching toward the railroad and beyond.

He knew the map to be correct in this. He had seen it at other times while riding the train.

Somewhere along the rail line up there was the Southern

Pacific water stop at Sentinel, a clutch of wood shacks and the one-room station, with a few paloverdes for shade.

There was the water tank, and a coaling shed and a section house, and that was all.

He wondered if that was Fannin's destination.

It was something to keep in mind.

But it was his intention to take them before they got there.

With that thought, he unconsciously began to push the horse. The mount, a blue roan, went easily on the downgrade from the pass.

And, once the basin flat was reached, he put it to a trot.

But the heat brought a quick lather, and he soon slowed. He'd take his chances on getting them in the Craters. He wasn't a man to abuse a horse.

There was a trail from the pass that had seen occasional use, and the convicts were sticking to it, obviously eager to reach the Craters and whatever relief they would afford.

The day grew into one of those that seemed bent on setting a record for heat. As the afternoon sun got lower, its burn got fiercer.

He was glad he had stopped pushing the roan. It could have been a fatal mistake, he thought.

Impatience was a fault that had killed many a horse. And had killed many a man as well.

Particularly in this part of the Territory.

Fannin would know this, too. He would not kill their horses by pushing either.

Fannin might not even know he was on their trail.

Neither would Opal. What would she be thinking?

Would she be hoping he was? Or hoping he wasn't?

Somehow, he guessed, this would depend on the treatment given her by Fannin.

CHAPTER 14

TWO hours later, he reached a ravine that led into the Crater foothills.

Bare sand and rock soon gave way to brush-covered slopes, but the heat remained. As the trail climbed, the brush gave way to chaparral; and higher up he could see patches of timber, and above that still-higher ridges.

Up there somewhere, I'll overtake them, he thought.

By the time he reached the first timber the westering sun had thrown deep shadow onto the trail, which here crossed a narrow, grassy meadow.

He shared what remained of his water with the roan, hobbled it to graze, ate a cold meal, and as darkness fell rolled up in the saddle blanket just within a bordering of pines.

After the heat of the desert, he felt an early chill, and slept only fitfully. He was not displeased by this—in periods of wakefulness he checked on the horse and listened for sounds of possible prowlers. He assumed Fannin was armed now. That friend of his with the robbers would have seen to that.

His final awakening came before first light. He arose, got the horse and saddled it, and found some beef jerky in his saddlebags.

He made that his breakfast, and hit the trail right after.

Ahead he could see where the thin graze had been trod by the pair's horses. He was surprised they had not made camp here, until he remembered they would have passed an hour earlier than he. There had been much more of daylight then.

The flat valley led to a draw, which in turn flared into

another similar one. He began to wonder if there was a chain of them perhaps, forming a lengthy pass through the range.

Then, abruptly, he came to the valley's end and faced a granite cliff. To the right was a steeply rising ravine into which the trail disappeared.

He hesitated, considering the risk of entering it. It provided a great place for an ambush, he thought.

Then, seeing no other way, he fisted his six-gun, kicked the roan's flanks, and began a twisting climb, trying to keep his eyes on what lay ahead.

At each turn he half expected a volley to knock him out of the saddle, and even in the cooler morning air, sweat covered his face.

He kept thinking: *Fannin is missing a good bet here; he must be concentrating on flight.*

Or does he know of a better spot to attack me?

Whatever the reason, he got through the ascending ravine without mishap.

Then, just as he emerged, a bullet struck the granite wall an arm's reach to his right. He heard it whine off in ricochet even as the report reached him from the fired weapon a couple of hundred yards away.

Maybe farther, he thought instantly. At two hundred yards, he would not have expected Fannin to miss.

He backed the roan down the defile and slid from the saddle.

Dropping the reins, he crept back up to peer from a meager cover of fallen boulders. He could see no sign of either Fannin or Opal, and was puzzled when no more shots were fired.

It made little sense to him. Fannin, he thought, was a better marksman than that. Hell, he'd shot the heel off Conley's boot back at the Tinajas Altas.

Fannin cursed.

He had been watching their backtrail periodically, and had

seen the top of Conley's hat appear in the defile, and, surprised, grabbed at the rifle given him by Slade, twisted, and fired while still mounted.

And at that moment, Opal drove her horse into his, making him miss.

Before he could fire again, she grabbed at his sleeve and jerked it.

By then his target had disappeared.

"Damn you!" he said, then wheeled his mount and drove it into a fringe of pines beside the trail.

She followed.

"What the hell did you do that for?" he said.

She said, "If you kill him, you and I are through."

"Are you insane? It's our chance to get free."

"Can't we just keep ahead of him?"

He swore again. "How? He's probably on a fresher horse. He must be, or he wouldn't have gained on us. We couldn't even see him until now."

"Even so," she said.

"What does that mean?"

She made no answer. She didn't know what she meant herself.

"Listen," he said, "you can't have it both ways. It's either him or us."

"He wouldn't kill us," she said.

"Maybe not you," he said. "But he'd damn sure kill me if he had to."

"Shoot his horse," she said. "But not him."

He stared at her. Then he nodded. "All right," he said.

He didn't say anything more then. He just looked back at the defile where he knew Conley was still hid.

"He won't come out now," she said. "And we can't just stay here waiting."

"Reckon you're right," he said. "We'll ride on. But next time I'll be shooting for the horse, like you want. So don't go spoiling my aim again."

She didn't reply. She thought, *How will I know what he'll be aiming at?*

I won't.

She looked back as they skirted through the timber. She saw no sight of Conley. He'd wait a while before leaving cover, she suspected. He'd wait until he'd given them time to move on, if that was to be their decision.

They reached another rise before Fannin halted, and leaving his mount in the trees, moved to where he could again study their backtrail.

"Stay hid," he'd told her, and she did. It bothered her that she was reaching a point where she obeyed his commands.

When he returned to her, he remounted and said, "A straight view there, clear back to that ravine. And no sight of him."

"He will keep coming," she said.

"Sure," he said. "All we got out of that shooting was a little delay."

She could sense his rancor coming back. He wasn't one to forget a gripe. She half expected him to berate her again, and was surprised when he didn't.

Instead, after they had ridden a while, he said, "You told me you know Colorado. That you know ranch life, too."

"Yes. I grew up there."

"We could go there," he said. "Start over."

"We?"

"Together. Start a new life."

"How?"

"Start a ranch of our own."

"With what?" she said.

"Hell, plenty of cowmen have started their own herds with rustled stock."

"Right back to the old life for you, isn't it?"

"No," he said. "Before, I was in it for the quick dollar. Steal them and sell them." He paused. "Now I'd be ready to settle down."

He had ridden close to her, and now he reached out and laid a hand on her arm.

"With you," he said.

She looked at him, saw what was in his eyes, and was wrenched by what she saw. He was serious.

She said, "Oh, Sam! It could never be. Don't you know that?"

"But it could!" he said. "I know it could."

She slowly shook her head.

"You think on it," he said. "We got a ways to go before you got to decide."

She said, "Sam, Sam." She had never called him by name before.

"I want you," he said. "More than you know."

She stared at the trail ahead. She did not want to face him when he said that.

"I grew up on a Kansas farm," he said. "Owned by a cousin of my old man. My folks died of some disease I don't remember when I was about seven. All I remember is back-breaking chores until I was fifteen. I run off then, come to the Territory and fell in with a wild bunch. Learned the rustling trade from them."

She listened in silence.

"I never give a thought before to settling down," he said. "So you must be the reason."

"Please, Sam. Don't talk about it now."

"I wanted you to know," he said. "I want you to think about it."

"So now you've told me," she said. "But now we have to think about getting away."

"If you don't interfere again, we will."

"Then you shoot his horse, not him."

"I said I would."

"How can I be sure?" she said.

"You promise to go with me, that's how," he said. The idea

seemed to grow on him then. "You promise, and I'll go for the horse. Otherwise . . ."

"I promise," she said.

He gave her one of his rare smiles. "You won't be sorry, Opal." It was the first time he'd called her anything but "girl."

Conley came out of his cover after a considerable wait. A man being pursued in rough country had the advantage over the one pursuing, as he knew from experience.

It had been unfortunate, his not overtaking Fannin in the open desert, but something that could not be helped if he valued not destroying the roan.

Now, though, he had lost part of the gain he had made over the long miles of the chase.

But he had to move cautiously here to avoid another ambush attempt. His frustration grew. It had been too much time since this job had begun. He had lost track of the number of days since he'd taken up the trail back at the prison.

He felt an urgency to get done with the chore, and that he knew could drive him to recklessness.

And yet there was always with him a reluctance to face up to what he must do with Opal. A reluctance caused by a hard decision heretofore unknown to him.

Always before, he had followed a rule that black was black and white was white where the law was concerned. But in her case he found himself in a fog of gray. It disturbed him. It had disturbed him from the beginning.

And now, as he saw the end was coming, one way or another, the disturbance had become acute.

It was a disturbance that was fueling a recklessness he had not felt since those early days as a youthful town marshal. Back when he'd lost Kate.

Later, he'd heard an old sheriff once say, "Son, there are

old lawmen and there are bold lawmen, but there are damn few old, bold lawmen."

The words had pretty well guided the conduct of his career.

Until now.

In a sudden surge of wildness, he kicked the blue roan's flanks and went into a trot. The hell with it, he thought. He'd run Fannin down and get it over with. Even if he had to draw hot lead again to do it.

It was Opal, glancing back, who glimpsed Conley in the screening of growth along a portion of the now winding and climbing trail. He appeared much nearer than she would have expected.

She stifled her first impulse to cry out a warning to Fannin, who had pulled slightly ahead as the trail narrowed.

Then, in a contradiction of feeling, she faced forward and said to him, "He's back there."

He twisted in his saddle, saying, "I know that."

"I mean he's close now. As close as he was at the ravine."

He halted, and turned his horse. "Where?"

"Down the trail there."

"How far?"

"Three hundred yards, maybe. Can you hit his horse at that distance?"

"Pull off here," he said. "I'll wait until he's closer to make sure."

When she was slow to act, he said, "Come on!" and rode into a mixed cover of trees and chaparral, scantier here due to a stretch of rocky soil. Still it afforded as good conceal-ment as any directly ahead.

"Get down," he said as he dismounted. "Tie up here and keep hid."

He took a crouching position, sighting down the trail. With the mounts secured, she joined him.

She said nervously, "Remember your promise."

"I ain't forgetting," he said.

"Can he see us?"

"I don't think so. The cover ain't that thin."

She could not let her anxiety rest. "If you want me," she said, "don't hurt him."

"Goddammit!" he said. "I told you I understood."

Conley appeared then, riding around a bend in the trail, coming on with a boldness that surprised her.

It must have surprised Fannin too, because he said, "Damn fool!" even as he brought up his weapon and aimed.

At a hundred and fifty yards, he fired.

She saw Conley jerk in his saddle, saw a red spot blossom on the shoulder of his shirt, saw him tumble from the saddle as his spooked horse plunged into a growth of juniper and disappeared.

Fannin fired again into the growth with a searching shot.

She leaped upon him from behind.

The jerk of his finger triggered another shot as he turned on her with a swinging left backhand that knocked her sprawling.

"You goddamn bitch!" he said.

She lay stunned, but said, "That wound was no accident!"

"How do you know?"

"I know."

"I should have known better," he said. "I should have known for sure what I always suspected. It's him you want."

He was facing her now. The rage in his face frightened her.

He turned away, looking down at where Conley was no longer in sight.

Then, abruptly, as she got to her feet, he turned back to her, took a quick step forward, and hooked his left fist against her jaw, knocking her down again.

He stood over her then, staring down at her, his rage leaving as he met her eyes. He seemed to have forgotten about Conley lying down below, wounded or dead.

His voice was choked when he spoke. "Oh, God, girl, I'm sorry! I lost my head. I never wanted to hurt you. Never!"

A shot came from below, whipping through the foliage above, tearing loose a branch that dropped on him.

His manner changed still again. He said, "You stay here. Keep down. It's me or him now."

Before she could protest, he was gone, disappeared into the chaparral.

Conley lay where he fell, feeling the hurt of his wound, feeling the blood run down his left arm.

He lifted himself enough to see through his concealment up to the likely spot from where the shots had come. He was in time to see Fannin rise from his own cover and to move toward Opal, and to see Fannin knock her down.

He had his six-gun free of his holster now, and snapped off a shot in quick anger. He judged he missed, although the convict disappeared.

Now, he thought, *each knows where the other is.*

Now it will be a stalking game.

He wadded up his neckerchief and stuffed it into the shoulder of his shirt, hoping it would stanch the flow of blood. Probing with his fingers, he judged the bullet had taken a chunk out of his flesh but passed by. The pain made him clench his teeth, but he could still move his arm.

He started working his way upward through the chaparral toward where he had glimpsed Fannin strike the girl.

He wondered about what he'd seen. The rustler was erratic in his moods, but using a fist on Opal was surprising, he thought. She must have done something to arouse him to rage. He tried to guess what it could be.

It came to him then that she might have tried to protect him, Conley. That she might have done the same previously, back at the ravine.

If so, how many times did it make that she had interfered to save his life? It was getting to be a habit.

And, as always when he thought about her, it made him uneasy.

A bullet striking granite nearby brought his mind back to the business at hand.

Rifle shot, he thought. Well, he had his own rifle in his hands, as well as his six-gun in his holster. In this close kind of encounter, the handgun might be more useful.

He stared up the chaparraled slope, in the direction of that last shot. There was just enough rise that he could see wisps of powder smoke shredded by the foliage as it rose toward the sky.

He did not return the shot. Instead, he plunged into the growth ahead and drove himself forward. Almost at once he felt the strength going out of his legs.

His movement had loosened the neckerchief over his wound; he could feel the blood running down the length of his upper arm. That, he knew, accounted for his sudden weakness. He'd have to go easy. Above all, he'd have to stay conscious. If he passed out now, Fannin would find him and kill him.

Conley crawled, crawled on his knees, trying to hold the rifle, but the strength went out of his left arm and he dropped it. He lost his balance and pitched forward.

Using his good right hand, he pushed himself up and felt dry leaves sticking to the sweat on his face.

He kept going, using his feet and his knees and his one good arm. He left the rifle behind where it had fallen.

He still had his revolver; he could feel the weight of it on his hip. There was a holding strap over the butt of it. He hoped it did not come loose. He did not reach to check it. He needed his right hand to open a way through the thick underbrush now surrounding him.

Where was Fannin now? Still up there? Waiting for him to expose himself?

He hoped not. He hoped Fannin was crawling through the damned chaparral, even as he was, because he feared that his waning strength would keep him from reaching Fannin otherwise.

In the thick growth, though, they might crawl past each other, and wouldn't that be ironic as hell, he thought.

And then, distracted by the weakness from his wound, he blundered out into a small clearing.

Too late, he saw Fannin five yards away on the opposite side, just visible through the foliage.

Still on his knees, he grabbed at his holster, jerked loose the holding strap, and drew.

Even as he lifted the gun, he saw the surprise on Fannin's face as he spotted Conley.

Fannin's rifle was held under his armpit, and he made no try to aim it. He fired a frantic shot and missed.

As he grabbed to lever the Winchester, Conley took quick aim and shot him near the heart.

Fannin dropped his rifle. He made no effort to pick it up. He crawled out of the brush and pitched forward into the clearing.

Conley held his weapon loosely, but did not fire again. He fell back to rest against the weak support of the brush behind him. He felt drained out. He kept staring at Fannin, wondering if he was dead.

Then Fannin lifted his head and looked at Conley with dulling eyes.

"You son of a bitch!" he said. "You'll take her back to prison, won't you?"

Conley made no answer.

She made her way down through the chaparral to where the exchange of shots had sounded. She had waited five minutes, ten minutes for more to come, then could wait no longer.

It was over now, she knew.

Down there, one or the other was dead. One or the other, or both.

Oh, God, let the one I want survive! she thought.

She struggled through the undergrowth and came upon the clearing, and cried out in dismay.

Conley was slumped unmoving, half hid by leafy branches. His eyes held a fixed stare at nothing. Congealing blood had darkened half of his shirt.

She began to cry.

And then, taken by a sudden chill, her glance swept across the clearing and found the body of Fannin sprawled with his face buried in a carpeting of leaves.

Both of them, she thought.

Both of them!

And then Conley's voice reached her. "He's dead," he said.

CHAPTER 15

THEY found a spring a little ways along the trail.

And there they camped for three days.

She cleaned his wound, and dressed it with strips torn from his now washed shirt, and it began to quickly heal.

It was an idyllic setting for them after the rigors of the desert trails.

They ate sparingly of their remaining supplies, postponing somewhat the need to move on.

He mentioned this to her on the second day.

"You are feeling better," she said. "There must be game here. Perhaps tomorrow you can hunt."

"Maybe," was all he said.

For two nights they slept, wrapped in their saddle blankets, a few feet apart.

But by the following day she could sense his vigor was returning, and though they continued to rest, she kept feeling his stare appraising her.

Once, in late afternoon, she caught his stare and held it until finally he dropped his own.

He got up restlessly from where he'd been lounging. "I'll see if I can find some game," he said.

It was near dusk when he returned with a couple of rabbits.

"Slim fare," he said. "But it's the best I could do."

They roasted them on sticks, and made do.

"Tomorrow we'll be leaving," he said.

It was the words she had been dreading to hear.

"All right," she said.

She studied his face in the flickering firelight. He was a man who had weathered much for his years, she thought.

And then the feeling toward him that she had first experienced back when he'd visited her at that cell in Florence came flooding over her, much stronger now. Made stronger by all they had been through together these past days.

Without a word, she arose and dragged her blanket over next to his.

He watched her in silence, meeting her eyes as she lowered herself beside him.

"Are you sure of this?" he said.

"Yes, Ridge," she said. "I'm sure."

He reached out and swept her against him, favoring only slightly his left arm.

For a long time he held her thusly, as her own hands caressed him.

And then they were stripping down to make love.

They made it insatiably, in near-continuous abandonment. The cookfire died down, and they kept at it in the dark.

Until, at last, he could go no more.

She lay then, replete and satisfied, beside him, his right arm pillowing her head.

He broke a long silence at last. "I don't understand," he said. "You were married once to Hartman."

"Yes," she said.

"How can it be, then?"

"That you found me a virgin?"

"Yes."

"Hartman could never consummate our marriage. That's what broke us up."

He was silent then, again. He seemed to be pondering the strangeness of what had happened.

As was she.

CHAPTER 16

IN the morning they descended the north slope of the Craters to the final desert, a flat, baked plain of scrub brush without so much as cactus visible.

They rode side-by-side, in silence, Conley leading the horse that Fannin had ridden.

She could not understand his silence at first, after what had happened between them the night before.

Once, she tried to break it, asking, "What lies ahead?"

He said shortly, "Sentinel Station. On the railroad."

That wasn't the answer she had been seeking by her question, and she was about to tell him so, until she saw the set, troubled expression of his face and thought better of it.

And then the haunting fear began to grow on her, and she was afraid to know the answer he might make if she pressed him.

So she did not ask again. But now her own expression became a match for his.

My God! she thought. *He couldn't!*

The heat was bad, rebounding from the nearly barren sand as the day wore on. So bad that in her misery she lost her fear—almost.

Once, they crossed an alkali-white *playa* where the sun's glare was so blinding that she rode with her eyes closed.

And then, past noon, they could see in the distance a dark line of what could be trees.

To her, it appeared as an oasis.

Even then he did not speak.

But it had to be Sentinel, she thought.

It was farther away than she had guessed. But eventually

she could make out the few wood structures against a line of palo verdes.

And presently she could identify them as a small station house, a section house, a coaling shed. And adjacent to the rails, a water tower.

So much for Sentinel, she thought. She remembered, now, passing through that other time. With a Pinal County deputy sheriff. On her way to Yuma.

And now her dread returned.

They pulled up beside the little station, and tied the horses. He held open the door, and gestured her in ahead of him.

He went up to the counter. He was again wearing his lawman's star.

He said, "Ridge Conley, Deputy U.S. marshal."

The Southern Pacific agent was a middle-aged man with a pale face and a green eyeshade.

He appeared startled. "Conley?" he said. "Conley! Aren't you the one they sent after—"

"Yeah," Conley said.

The S.P. man's glance went to Opal. "That's her?"

"Yeah."

"Hell, we heard you were down in the Gran Desierto."

"I was," Conley said.

The agent kept staring at her. She stared back.

"Where's the other two?" the agent said.

"Dead."

The S.P. man's eyes flicked back to the marshal. There was a quick excitement showing in them. "You had to kill them, hey?"

"Something like that," Conley said.

A different kind of excitement showed suddenly. "And you been traveling with her alone all these days." The agent gave Opal another lingering appraisal. Whatever he was thinking, he did not put it into words.

"I need transportation to Yuma," Conley said.

"Sure thing, Marshal. You got the fare?"

"I got three horses outside."

"I'm not allowed to barter for fares," the station man said.

"I don't mean to trade them. I've got the fare. I want to leave the horses for a couple of days."

"Might be a little feed and some grain in the section house. We keep some on hand in case somebody in the outlying area wants to ship an animal or two now and then."

Conley gestured at the telegraph key. "Wire your agent at Yuma. Ask him to send word to the prison for somebody to come down the hill to pick us up."

"I guess I can do that."

"Do it, then," Conley said. "When does the westbound come through?"

The agent looked at his watch. "Be along in fifty-nine minutes," he said. "Arrives here at five twenty-five. Will arrive Yuma eight-oh-one. You timed it pretty well, Marshal. You must be running in luck."

Conley gave him a long, tortured stare, saying nothing.

The S.P. man squirmed under it and turned to his telegraph key.

CHAPTER 17

THE westbound came through on time and was stopped by the S.P. agent to let them board.

He stood by as they climbed the steps to the coach's vestibule.

"Good luck, Marshal," he said.

Conley seemed not to hear him.

"And to you, ma'am," the agent said.

She looked at him to see if he was joking, and when she saw he meant it, she said, "For what?"

He looked confused, and said, "Well, ma'am, I don't rightly know. . . ."

And then they disappeared into the coach, and he stood there, looking perplexed, and said to himself, "Damned if I do."

She stared out the window at the desert they had crossed that day. Conley had motioned her next to it, and had taken the aisle half of the seat for himself.

Almost at once he had pulled his hat brim low over his eyes, leaning his head back as if trying to doze, ignoring her completely.

She thought back to the Yuma arrival time given them by the station agent. Two and a half hours, or more, she thought. My God! Is he going to sleep through it—our last hours together?

She turned to him. "Ridge?"

He kept his eyes covered. "Yeah?"

"We've got to talk."

"About what?"

"About us, for God's sake!"

"Talk, then," he said.

"Look at me!"

He straightened in his seat, shoving back his hat, and faced her. "I'm sorry," he said.

"You're *sorry*? That's all you've got to say? *You're taking me back to prison!*"

"It isn't my willing," he said. "I wish it was otherwise. But it's something I have to do. And you've already done over a year of the five they gave you."

"Four more years! And Fannin said they'd add more for escaping."

"Maybe not," he said, but he knew she didn't believe him. "If I didn't take you in, you'd be a fugitive. On the run. And you'd sooner or later be caught by somebody."

"At least it wouldn't be you."

"It has got to be me," he said. "I was hoping you'd understand that."

She turned away from him and stared out the window again.

"Maybe I do," she said. "But it doesn't make it any easier."

He said, "I wish there was some way it did."

As the train pulled into the Yuma depot, Conley saw the same wagon and waiting teamster that had given him the ride up the hill less than two weeks before.

Two weeks? It seemed more like two months.

The old teamster sat unmoving on the seat of his empty supply wagon and watched them descend from the car's platform.

There was a small crowd of loafers watching too.

"That's them!" somebody said. "I seen her in Florence that time of the trial. That's the same marshal, too!"

The crowd started to push closer.

Conley moved fast, pulling her along, almost dragging

her. He thrust her up on the wagon seat and climbed up beside her.

"Let's go!" he said to the driver.

The old man got the team moving before he spoke. "Got her back, did you?"

Conley did not answer.

Opal stared ahead, saying nothing.

The driver studied her out of the corner of his eye.

"You look some the worse for wear, missy."

"Leave her alone," Conley said.

"Only trying to be friendly," the driver said. "She looks like she could use a friend."

"Just leave her alone," Conley said.

"Well, the prison superintendent will be happy. He'll be damn glad to see her."

Conley was silent again.

It was more than the oldster could stand. He said, "What I wonder, Marshal, is how you feel about it. I mean, bringing her back to live in one of them rock cages up there."

"I'm a lawman," Conley said. "How I feel has nothing to do with it."

That seemed to gripe the old man. "I guess when you pin on that star you start marching to a different drumbeat," he said.

He glanced at Opal and shook his head. "Was it me, and I was your age, I'd have kept on going with her down into old Méjico and never come back."

"Horny for your old age, aren't you?"

"Nope," the old man said. "But I damn well wish I was."

They reached the top of the bluff at the prison's end, and as they came around the corner, Conley could see the superintendent's cottage in the outer yard. That's where he'd been told to come.

His glance went across the yard then to rest on the sally

port in the prison wall. In the thick wall its rounded top gave it the look of a tunnel. A tunnel to hell, he thought.

The iron-stripped double gates were locked now. But they would open soon. And Opal would disappear within.

The old man saw the long stare Conley was giving those bars of iron.

He said, "It takes all kinds to make a world, I reckon. You going to get down, or just sit there staring?"

Superintendent Bates was in his residence office, waiting. He stepped out on the porch as he heard the wagon drive up.

"Been expecting you," he said. "Stationmaster told me that you'd arrived."

He studied them, his glance switching from one to the other. Then he said, "Not a happy couple, it appears."

"What did you expect?" Conley said.

"I'd think you'd be pleased you got the job done. My congratulations. Too bad about the other two, but this was the one the administration worried about. Bad publicity about the system can cause problems for some people in high places."

"How high?" Conley said.

"How high?" Bates hesitated, then said, "The message I got was the governor himself was worried."

He turned to Opal. "You caused us a lot of trouble, young woman. You can expect some time in the snake den for it."

"Snake den?" Conley said. "The solitary confinement cell?"

Bates nodded, still watching Opal. "Blasted out of the rock-hard caliche. Only air and light from a small shaft drilled from the ceiling to the hilltop above. Blanket on the earth floor, a canteen of water, and a wood bucket for a privy." He paused. "Ten days or so of that, and she'll think twice about making more trouble for us."

"Listen," Conley said. "As a favor to me for bringing her back, don't put her in there."

"Well, well," Bates said.

"What do you mean by that?"

"You know what I mean, I think. Kind of grew on you, did she, Marshal?"

Conley didn't answer that. He said only, "I'm asking as a favor."

"Favor granted, because of what you did in tracking her down," Bates said. "But don't be sheepish about the way you feel, Marshal. Half my guards would like to roll her in the hay." He stopped suddenly, studying Conley's face. "Or in the sagebrush, for that matter."

"You insinuating something?" Conley said.

"I hope not!" Bates said. "What a hell of a newspaper story that would make!"

Opal had been listening, not saying a word.

Now she spoke up. "That would be a scandal, wouldn't it, Mr. Bates? Just what you and the governor and all the rest want to avoid?"

"Be the marshal's word against yours," Bates said, frowning. He turned to Conley. "One thing I've learned for sure since I've been here. Women convicts in a basically men's prison are one hell of a nuisance."

Conley said, "There's some other things I want to bring up."

"What things?" Bates said.

"Extenuating circumstances. I'll list them in my full report, of course. But this girl saved my life a couple of times, even though she knew I'd bring her in."

"Go on."

"Briefly, she warned me against an attack by a former partner of Fannin's named Kuster, and I managed to gun him down. Later, when we were under attack by a Mex bandido in Caborca, she saved me again."

The superintendent looked at Opal with a different interest. He said to her, "Why, girl?"

She did not answer at once. Then she said, "It seemed the right thing to do."

Bates appeared thoughtful. Finally, he said, "I'll submit the marshal's report to the governor's board of prison commissioners. Your actions in the marshal's behalf may be weighed against the additional term levied on you for escaping. Beyond that, I can promise you nothing."

She showed him no expression.

Conley said, "She saved my life!"

"As I said, her efforts will be considered. Possibly the added time will be dropped completely."

"Goddammit!" Conley said. "That still leaves her with almost four years to do!"

The superintendent gave him a long, level look. "You knew that when you brought her back here, didn't you, Marshal?"

Conley bid her good-bye at the women's yard of the prison, while the Mexican women watched interestedly and somewhat smirkingly.

Riding the train back to Casa Grande, he could still hear the clang of the iron-barred gates as they slammed behind him when he left.

Conley waited to hear, from Bates, the reaction of the prison commissioners to his report.

When it came, he cursed them all, long and loud. *The unfeeling sons of bitches!* And he cursed himself. *That goddamn star had brought him to this!*

He paced the floor of his office throughout a sleepless night.

At dawn he sat at his desk and began to write a letter:

Ridge Conley
Deputy U.S. Marshal
Florence, Arizona Territory
October 15, 1888

Alexander Johnson,
Governor
Prescott, Arizona

Dear Governor:
I have just been advised by superintendent Robert Bates of the Territorial Prison, in regard to the case of Opal Hartman who I returned to the prison a couple of months ago, that despite her saving my life on at least two occasions, thus sacrificing her own chance to remain free, she will continue to be incarcerated for the nearly four years of her original sentence.

Although Bates assures me that a copy of my report, in which I described her courageous and self-sacrificing actions, was sent to you, I want to emphasize here again that I would not be alive today, was it not for her.

Nor would she be behind bars.

Therefore, I am making this pesonal plea to you for clemency for her.

I am enclosing again a detailed description of the extenuating circumstances of her actions for you to reconsider.

These are circumstances that I am certain would impress the territorial newspapers, if I should go to them with my story.

Hoping to see justice done,

Ridge Conley

Conley hated making the threat but, by God, he *would* go to the newspapers to tell of Opal's heroic actions if Governor Johnson failed to listen to reason. It might cost Conley his job, but the hell with it.

He not only owed his life to Opal—he loved her, and had ever since that time in the Craters. He had brought her in anyway because a man had to play the hand dealt him, he thought. Even the rustler Fannin believed that. A man had his code, and if he was a man he lived by it, no matter what the cost.

Especially if he wore the lawman's star.

Within days of receiving Conley's letter, the Governor got an unexpected correspondence from Superintendent Bates:

> *Robert L. Bates*
> *Superintendent,*
> *Arizona Territorial Prison*
> *October 22, 1888*

Alexander Johnson
Governor,
Territory of Arizona

Honorable Sir:
This is a follow-up letter after my report of late July, which you will recall concerned the recapture of the female inmate, Opal Hartman.

I enclose a medical report by our prison physician, Dr. Niles Lenniger, pertaining to the condition of this woman who, as you know, has been in recent past of considerable concern to myself, the prison commissioners, and yourself. As you will see by Dr. Lenninger's report, he has diagnosed her to be with child.

In a prison filled with male convicts (and guards!) I feel we have here a situation that can be pounced upon by a scandal-mongering press. A situation that can bring nothing but tarnish to those of us in authority, and possibly to your own political career.

My concern is due primarily to the critical attention toward us by newspaper journalists unduly fascinated by her charismatic demeanor, in spite of the charge on which she was convicted.

I therefore beseech you to consider an early parole for Convict Hartman, early enough to preclude her condition becoming apparent here, thus avoiding further embarrassment to us all.

Your Obedient Servant,

Robert L. Bates

Ridge Conley waited in the outer yard, seated on the supply wagon driven by the old teamster.

Superintendent Bates himself escorted Opal to the sally port, where they waited until the turnkey unlocked the gates.

As they emerged, Ridge jumped down and strode toward them, and took the small handbag of her belongings from her.

They walked together toward the waiting wagon, leaving Bates standing alone in silence, staring after them with a thoughtful frown on his face.

As Ridge handed her up to the seat, Opal stared back at Bates. She lifted her hand in a gesture of good-bye.

Bates did not wave back.

The old teamster started the team and turned the wagon out onto the prison road before he glanced sidewise at the pair.

Then he said, "Heading for the depot?"

"Yes," Conley said.

"You make a compatible-looking couple," the oldster said.

"I hope so," Opal said.

"Being a husband and father," Conley said, "is going to be something new to me."

Opal reached over then and touched his hand.

If you have enjoyed this book and would like to receive details of other Walker Western titles, please write to:

Western Editor
Walker and Company
720 Fifth Avenue
New York, NY 10019